# *Creative Writing From Middlesex 2001*

Edited by Lucy Jeacock

First published in Great Britain in 2001 by
*YOUNG WRITERS*
Remus House,
Coltsfoot Drive,
Peterborough, PE2 9JX
Telephone (01733) 890066



HB ISBN 0 75432 370 6
SB ISBN 0 75432 371 4

# *FOREWORD*

This year Young Writers proudly presents a showcase of the best 'A Day In The Life Of . . .' short stories, from up-and-coming writers nationwide.

To write a short story is a difficult exercise. Much imagination and skill is required. *A Day In The Life Of . . . Creative Writing From Middlesex 2001* achieves and exceeds these requirements. This exciting anthology will not disappoint the reader.

The thought, effort, imagination and hard work put into each story impressed us all, and again, the task of editing proved demanding due to the quality of entries received, but was nevertheless enjoyable.

We hope you are as pleased as we are with the final selection and that you continue to enjoy *A Day In The Life Of . . . Creative Writing From Middlesex 2001* for many years to come.

# *CONTENTS*

Barham Primary School

| | |
|---|---|
| Priya Patel | 1 |
| Rebecca Milsome | 2 |
| Hira Cheema | 3 |
| Hollie Tarala Patel | 4 |
| Mira Mulji | 5 |
| Dhiren Gami | 6 |
| Priya Gaglani | 7 |
| Neena Mistry | 8 |
| Robert Woodward | 9 |
| Arti Bhundia | 10 |
| Rupa Vara | 11 |
| Jyoti Varsani | 12 |
| Shinal Desai | 13 |
| Kinari Mehta | 14 |
| Radhika Kotecha | 15 |
| Martina O'Donnell | 16 |
| Cassandra Linton | 17 |
| Aman Abrol | 18 |
| Sonkia Rajput | 19 |

Bourne Primary School

| | |
|---|---|
| Tobi Otudeko | 20 |
| Leanne Retter | 21 |
| Toni Phillips | 22 |
| Anita Rajani | 23 |
| Samantha Pegram | 24 |
| Jack Stevenson | 25 |
| Sam Wilson | 26 |
| Rochelle Donaldson | 27 |
| Ian O'Connell | 28 |
| Zoë Long | 30 |
| Rebecca Barrowman | 31 |
| Samantha Rosario | 32 |
| Sukhina Sidhu | 33 |
| Alex Ormrod | 34 |

Leanne Phillips 35
Ben Rosendale 36
Victoria Leahy 37
Nick Glenday 38
Simone Monks 39
Arushi Gandhi 40
Mark Grimes 41
Alex Philpott 42
Andrew Nisbet 43
Zara Nogales 44
Monique Belgrave 46
Cristina Di Genua 47
Joe Bridle 48
Charlotte Moorse 49
Sean McShane 50
Kathleen Gray 51
Karl Graves 52
Sam Richardson 53
Hannah Constable 54
Sophie Kimmins 56
Scott Roberts 57
Samuel Spettigue 58
Grace Hennessy 60
Sophie Dalmedo 61

Field End Junior School

Cheryle Hall 62
Rhys Williams 63
Christopher Bolwell 64
Ceri Gordon 65
Nicole Panayi 66
Wilson Tang 67
Stephanie Worthy 68
Harry Saunders 69
Nirmal Trivedy 70
Jon Platt 71
Natasha Caine 72
Damian Holland 74

| | |
|---|---|
| Lauren Arnold | 76 |
| Josh O'Neill | 77 |
| Courtenay Hilmi | 78 |
| Katie Lecky | 80 |
| James King | 81 |
| Hayley Weaver | 82 |
| Oliver Michaelson | 84 |
| Nicola Bates | 85 |
| Alex Pearce | 86 |
| Laura Loxton | 88 |
| Ben Hunter | 89 |
| Peaches Demetriou | 90 |
| Sam Pearce | 91 |
| Ryan Endacott | 92 |
| Jessica Brownlee | 93 |
| James Bowers | 94 |
| Helen Gillen | 96 |
| Stuart Sims | 97 |
| Jack Aylott | 98 |
| Matt Berryman | 99 |
| Priscilla Lok | 100 |
| Stephen Murton | 102 |
| Emma Rigg | 103 |
| Charlotte Baker | 104 |
| Matthew Ayling | 105 |
| Paul Goodey | 106 |
| Jessica Williams | 107 |
| Philip Upton | 108 |
| Rebecca Simmons | 109 |
| Alex Rostocki | 110 |
| Billy Evans | 111 |
| Lucy Wilson | 112 |
| Omari Elliott | 113 |
| Zara Sellars | 114 |
| Hannah Wood | 115 |
| Sophia Pope | 116 |
| Amy Thomas | 118 |
| Sasha Nurse | 119 |

Charlotte Lawrence 120
Michael Lee 122
Emma Freebody 124
James Wolman 126
Melissa Holland 127
Mauro Urgo 128
Nik Mills 129
Hayley Marr 130
Rachel Lehane 131
Rebecca Lanning 132
Tom King 133
Rhoswyn Heale 134
Katie Fulbrook 135
Chelsey Costello 136
Thomas Clissold 138
Emily Begner 139
Kelly Smith 140
Hayley Kennedy 141
Amanda Bonnar 142
Dominic Brall 143
Samantha Jones 144

Longfield Middle School

Sarah Chisholm 145
Kelly Hoskins 146
Amy Tribbick 148
Nicholas Todd 150
Hollie Glazebrook 151
Shefali Shah 152
Priya Raja 153
Christopher Henson 154
Robert Brown 156
John Vinton 157
Anish Bhagat 158
April Sullivan 159
Nicholas Margalski 160
Pavetha Seeva 161
Rushil Vithlani 162

Roma Tournier-Blake 163
Saher Gardezi 164
Laura Bodimeade 165
Neima Said 166
Nicole Gibbs 167
Safoora Kamal 168
Daveena Patel 169
Sara Harman 170
Jade Priest Hurley 171
Zarina Ilyas 172
Amrit Mahbubani 173
Gurpreet Tatla 174
Jaspal Singh Tatla 175
Thomas Watson 176
Grant Fynn 178
Michael Tredgett 179
Pallavi Gajjar 180
Nina Parmar 181

Priestmead Middle School

Kaiya Chowdhary 182
Alison Faconti 183
Katherine Franks 184
Rajenthini Varadarajah 185
Samil Shah 186
Luke Peters 187
Shweta Dattani 188
Samina Omar 189
Kushal Shah 190
Todd Davies 191
Nilma Shah 192
Aaron Gilchrist 193
Rowena Shah 194
Menisha Chauhan 195
Tomos Jones 196
Kishan Sitapara 197
Krishen Shah 198
Heeral Shah 199

St Lawrence RC School, Feltham

| | |
|---|---|
| Thomas Owen | 200 |
| Linno Soares | 201 |
| Joshua Ssali | 202 |
| Joseph Everett | 203 |
| Jack Devereux | 204 |
| Aaron O'Sullivan | 205 |
| Natalina Fashoda | 206 |
| Kathryn Mellon | 207 |
| Florence Proctor | 208 |
| Debora Lopes | 209 |
| Jamie Barlow | 210 |
| Rachel Welch | 211 |
| Rachel Haldane | 212 |
| Christie Braham | 213 |
| Jessica Browne | 214 |
| Luke Taylor | 215 |
| Francesca Barry | 216 |
| Amber-Rose Cox | 217 |
| Estelle Johnson | 218 |

Saxon Primary School

| | |
|---|---|
| Mark Davies | 219 |
| Greg Stabler | 220 |
| Charlie Cusack | 221 |
| Alicia Irwin | 222 |
| Lui Matthews | 223 |
| Kelly Harris | 224 |

# *The Stories*

## Day In The Life Of A Victorian Child

I have to go to work every day. We are poor people. I am five years old. I have to work to clean chimneys and my friend got stuck and he died. It was very sad. Every day I get up at 5.00am. It takes me 30 minutes to get there as I have to walk 9km. If you come late you get whipped. I went up the chimney and my legs got scraped against the wall and they started to bleed. When someone does not come out, they light the fire so they get out of the chimney,

The boss was strict he always wanted his own way. They put salt water on the cuts to stop the bleeding. We get 30 minutes tea break every day. We work 13½ hours a day. and we get home at 9.00pm. For dinner we get milk, bread, rice and meat to eat. We have a small home. It is made out of straw and mud. We did not have money to paint it. I get paid 3p a day, that was a lot for us. We sleep on the floor.

I had a sister and I was the oldest. You can see a little boy sleeping on the floor with no blanket. Some were starving, they were all skinny because they did not get enough food. I have never got stuck in the chimney. Lucky for me!

***Priya Patel (11)***
***Barham Primary School***

## A Day In The Life Of A Vacuum Cleaner

Hi, good morning! My name is Vacuum Cleaner. My life is very interesting. I'm a very hardworking piece of machinery. I can't tolerate any rubbish on the floor. I normally stay in the small room. My master's name is John. He loves cleanliness and I'm one of his favourite things to clean with.

One day it happened that it was John's birthday and he had invited quite a few friends. Obviously the whole house had to be very thoroughly cleaned. John put a new bag in and started cleaning the living room. But all of a sudden I heard a cracking noise and my machinery stopped. John opened me up and checked very carefully to find out what had gone wrong with me. John also checked for a fuse in my plug as well, but it was OK. He tried his best but he could not fix me, so he took me to the proper electrical engineer. He also opened most of my parts and surprisingly he found a screw which was stuck and had broken one of the parts. This part was very important and to get it repaired was very expensive. John's friend suggested to dump me and buy another vacuum cleaner. Oh my God, I was so shocked. I didn't even dream of that! I will be thrown away in the skip. But I knew that John really wouldn't throw me away.

He said 'No, I don't want any other vacuum cleaner! Then he got me repaired and took me home with the new part. I was cleaning even better than before. John is very happy with me and I still remember that day of my life.

***Rebecca Milsome (11)***
***Barham Primary School***

## A Day In The Life Of A Victorian Child

I woke up sweating with fear, for the nightmares I'd had weren't very pleasant. They were re-enacting the night my hand got cut off by a wagon roaming around. I got up at the speed of light from the doorstep I'd been sleeping on and headed towards the coal mine as fast as my legs could carry me.

As soon as I got there, the boss shouted orders at everyone. He's is probably the biggest brute in London, he's selfish and cowardly. he loves ordering people around and gets paid for nothing.

I crawled to my square and started digging with more enthusiasm than normal. The boss just jumps at the sight of an innocent nine year old. When I grow up I'll be a manager and I'll treat workers just how boss treated us.

The mine was dark and dismal with no room for moving and hardly any room for breathing. After 12 hours of working and only eight or nine hours of sleeping, it seems like an instinct to go to sleep in the middle of work. But I wasn't going to make that dreadful mistake again. After all no human can stand more than one handless arm.

At dinner time we have one small piece of bread and a bowl of soup which explains my thin form and at the end of the gruelling day we get paid a measly 7 dimes (3p).

As soon as I got out of the mine I fell asleep against a tree, I shook with fear all night, dreading the forthcoming day.

***Hira Cheema (11)***
***Barham Primary School***

## A Day In The Life Of A Victorian Child

My name is Hollie, and I work as a coal miner, it's really difficult. It's not as if I have a choice. You see my mum doesn't get paid much more than I do and my dad was murdered. My mum doesn't let me say that in front of our bosses. My dad was whipped 500 times non-stop.

I would say it's about 12.30 in the afternoon and I've just had my lunch, which was only soup, bread and milk. For breakfast I had bread, boiled milk and oatmeal.

I leave home at around 4.30 in the morning to walk three stupid miles to a hot and dark pit and to be working at 7.00am at the latest, otherwise I get whipped and miss my excuse of a breakfast.

I used to have a friend called Jenny but the poor thing died on her last day there, (her father robbed his boss and had run off while he was asleep!) She got caught in an avalanche of coal and rubble, when my boss found out he just said, 'I would have paid you more if you were still alive!' Cruel, isn't it!

It's really hot and dark down here and I get really agitated, so agitated that I have snapped at my boss and to 'learn my lesson', he keeps me in till I've collected over a ton of coal.

My boss is a slave-driver and whenever he can, he will avoid paying you a measly 7d and I only realise once I've walked halfway home and of course I have to turn back otherwise we get thrown out of our home. (which is, may I remind you, a cold dormitory).

At the end of the day I eat bread and milk for dinner and head home.

***Hollie Tarala Patel (11)***
***Barham Primary School***

## Day In The Life Of A Victorian Child

I walked to my horrifying job, as a chimney sweep. I see my boss who gives me an evil sneer as I get my sweeper and begin to climb up the ladder. I get stuck and start to struggle. I heard my boss say, 'Get down or I'll light the flames!' I didn't answer. I saw flickering flames beneath me. The flames go bigger and bigger. I tried to climb out but I couldn't. I heard skin tearing off me as I began to haul myself up. I tried to think either to die or climb out and not have my dinner. I squeezed myself out of the chimney and began to take deep breaths as I inhaled oxygen.

'Why didn't you come out? For this, you are not going to get your dinner, which is really unlucky for you because you were going to get your favourite meal, meat, bread and porridge.'
'But Sir!' I said, 'I have been starving all day, can't I even get half a loaf?' I begged on my knees.
*'No!'* the cruel boss bellowed. I thought to myself, I have to suffer and all for what, 3p a day. I just wish I could go home.

***Mira Mulji (11)***
***Barham Primary School***

## A Day In The Life Of A Shoe

Hello, my name is Doc Martins and I'm a type of a shoe. I'm a hard-wearing resilient product of shoes and I have been bought for many years. I'm no good on slim feet but I fit huggingly well into broader feet. I'm made out of tough and stiff leather with a thick leather sole, which is heavy on my wearer's feet.

I kick-start my day by being worn by my owner Rocky Bellsprout. Every morning he lifts me out of my cold habitat, away from my friends and I have the pleasure of being worn by a warm, cotton fleshy foot.

Every morning I experience an adventurous journey through Nottingham forest, touching mud, gravel, pavement, leaves and sometimes unwanted 'waste' which leaves me deflated in my spirit. This journey leads me to Rocky's school, St Johns. I have a long rest during work time, but then have to start my job again at play, due to friction between my souls and the ground. My souls experience wear and tear, also I get cold and clammy from my wearer's sweat, but my resilient leather absorbs the moisture and then I'm comfortable. After the six hours of school, I am lead through that adventurous journey again.

Once I get home I'm normally lead to the garden to play a game called 'football' with his mates. Fortunately it was on a muddy ground so I didn't get hurt, but I sure did have a long game. By the time we finished, it was time for dinner for Rocky, so he took me off and I had a lovely nap in my cold habitat in the porch with my mates.

***Dhiren Gami (11)***
***Barham Primary School***

## A DAY IN THE LIFE OF A VICTORIAN CHILD

Oh, do I have to wake up? I hate waking up in the early morning. I'm sorry I'm muttering things to myself and I forgot to introduce myself.

Hi, I'm Jenny Benson age five. I live with my mother and father. I have to go to work every day.

It's 3.00am, well I better get dressed and ready to go to work. I leave at 4.00am and reach work at 6.00am and work finishes at 9.00pm. I reach home at 11.00pm and it's 24km altogether.

Here I am cleaning chimneys. I hate my boss, he's cruel and he whips me. 'Oi you brat, come out!' he says. Just now he lit a fire at the bottom. I screamed my head off when the boiling fire touched my foot. I had to crawl out with my arms and legs scraping against the bricks. I almost suffocated in there, there was no air. I have to eat only what the doctor says and it doesn't give me enough energy. For breakfast I had bread and milk. I better get back to work. Whoa that was close! That stone nearly hit my eye. I only get 4p a day. I'm fed up of working but at least it pays. Oh it's lunch! I had bread pudding and milk.

Now I have to clean another chimney, it's so dirty I'm completely covered in soot. Some children sleep on floors and doorsteps but I get to sleep with my parents.

It's supper! I had milk, oatmeal and bread. It's 8.50pm now, I'm feeling really tired. If I sleep I'll get whipped. Well time's up but I have to walk home.

***Priya Gaglani (11)***
***Barham Primary School***

## A Day In The Life Of A Victorian Child

I woke up at 5.30 in the morning stressed out because I have to work for ten hours a day. I was extremely tired and afraid with fear of going down to dig coal. I had to sleep outside in the cold where all the rich people live with fancy jewellery and clothes. I had to head for work at 6.30 and did not have breakfast because they just give you bread. I reached work and nearly got whipped because I was one minute late. I started to dig with no one around me apart from the old, mean stubborn man. I started digging and sweated and at last I found some coal but it was a stone. I dug for another twenty minutes and found coal. I was in such a state that I just had to have a bath. The old mean man gave me some bread, rice, milk and two pieces of meat. I stayed there for half an hour with soup in my hand. I then dug coal with all the dirt piling on top of me. I dug and dug and found no coal and it had been a hard day. James the boss told me to go. I looked and looked and found no place to sleep and then found an empty cardboard box.

***Neena Mistry (11)***
***Barham Primary School***

## A DAY IN THE LIFE OF A WALKING BOOT

Dear Diary,
I woke up at 5:30am as usual. But to my surprise everyone was up talking about the walk up Snowdon.
'Can I wear my walking boots?' said Robert.
'Of course you can, that's why we bought them,' said Alison.
I said to my friend Trainer 'Oh no not this again!' Trainer laughed.

The next thing I know I've got a smelly foot and thick sock in me and we were at the bottom of Snowdon. I wish we had taken the train at least one way. But they had to walk as it was illegal to take the train.

The ground was rough and slippery, they began to run and that gave me pins and needles. Sometimes I had to jump, sometimes I had to scramble and I slipped, nearly killing myself. At last we reached the summit and all that I could see were the laziest shoes who had been sleeping in the train. At last I could have rest.

I hated the next part because my foolish owners took the wrong route. We had to climb over the rockiest ground I have ever felt, even though I have climbed Ben Nevis in Scotland. We had to go through water to get to the other side and I was soaked. I needed the sun to come out but my wishes did not come true.

Just as I thought we were going to slow down, we sped up again. In fact we started to run to catch a bus.

Finally, we got back to the car and they started to take me off. 'Yes!' I was glad to know that I was going to have a rest. Now Trainer had to take over all the hard work and I laughed.

***Robert Woodward (10)***
***Barham Primary School***

## A DAY IN THE LIFE OF A VICTORIAN CHILD

I had just turned ten and my parents told me that I was going to earn a living, by going in a coal mine digging coal. They also told me that I would have to travel at least three miles a day. I felt as if I was made to be an adult at an early age of my life and felt terrible not knowing what I would experience from this.

The next day I woke at 5:00am so I could be there before 7:00am. I hate working in a coal mine, I keep slipping and now I've got cuts everywhere. Once I even got whipped for talking! The conditions are absolutely terrible! It's so dark and I get hot very easily.

Anyway, for breakfast they fed me dry bread and boiled milk which wasn't the very best but I was grateful. I worked twelve whole hours and if I broke any rules I would have to work another hour as my punishment.

At the end of the day my master would pay me three pence for the work. Some days my master would try to avoid paying me by putting coal and rubble in my bag, so by the time I reached home, I would have realised I was tricked and I would have to travel back to collect my money. Some days when my parents found out I had been tricked by my master, they would whip me for lying to them.

***Arti Bhundia (11)***
***Barham Primary School***

## A Day In The Life Of A Victorian Child

I wake up on a glistening day. The sun is shining, it is 4 o'clock. I know I have to go to people's houses to clean the mouldy and rusty looking awful chimneys for an hour or so. I see my ripped up crinkly clothes, so dirty and tattered. I see my head full of sweat and blood. I see so many rich people looking down at me as if I am something nobody has seen before. I can feel the breeze of the wind pulling me to a beautiful house. I clean the chimney, sweep, sweep, sweep! I can feel my bruises, so bumpy and huge. I fall asleep slowly, slowly but then the owner of the house comes and gets me up and beats me. I run, run, run away from the crazy old man. I fall to the ground and I see the big, bright moon. I see the stars. I die, peacefully, peacefully, peacefully. My life ends as a child. I thought I would become rich and live forever.

***Rupa Vara (11)***
***Barham Primary School***

## A Day In The Life Of A Victorian Child

'Wake up chimney boys, wake up chimney boys,'
I jolt and run to my boss. We pick up the other chimney boys and go to our chimneys. I say to myself, 'I have to go to that dark pit don't I?' I brush up and down and make every brick crystal clear. I have been working for four hours continuously.

I have an extra long break. I see a lofty man staring down at me while I look up at him. He has a cane in his hand, I feel the whip smack my hand *'Ahhhh'* I shout, holding my bare hands in front of me and there, a long mark of the cane printed on my hand.

I climb back to the black pit, I hear the echo of my crying inside. I see nothing but black. I carry on working until my boss says I can have my dinner.

I climb down the ladder, scratching my elbows and knees. I make my way to the dining room all covered in soot. I have a seat and Mrs Sue clashes my plate on the table. I get two peas, one carrot and a small, thin, mouldy slice of bread. That's all that was on my bare plate. I wish for a long meal.

I do the last bit at the bottom of the chimney. I finish at last and go home. It is dark outside, I cannot hear anything. I return to my alleyway and put the pile of newspaper on my feet and back to keep me warm.

***Jyoti Varsani (11)***
***Barham Primary School***

## A Day In The Life Of A Victorian Child
## Chimney Sweep

I climb what seems a never-ending ladder. Broom in hand, I dive legs first into the dark solitary chimney. I take a deep breath and start cleaning, so fast it'll make me dizzy. My throat dries as I inhale the floating smoke and soot. The scraping of the knees gets so bad they bleed. Fresh blood runs down my knees like the tears running down my cheeks. The sound *'lunch'* soothes my burning knees.

I eat my stale bread with sour milk. I climb the chimney once again, looking up at the distant opening. The light the floods in, it is almost refreshing. I can see a bird flying, it is so free and peaceful that I envy it. I fall down painfully to the bottom, there and then my boss beats me. I curl up in pain, emotions and anger running within tears.

Suddenly he stops, he's distracted, I run for my life. As I approach the alleyway a car knocks me over the rich passenger throws me 2p. As I lie there on the side of the road, limbs twitching and shuffling, I see people walking on the pavement, taking one glare and once again walking on, not even taking another glance. I struggle slowly to reach the alleyway where I rest knowing that this is the way I will live till I starve to death or get finished by my boss or maybe die by misery. As I close my eyes I know I've lived another day in this cruel life.

***Shinal Desai (11)***
***Barham Primary School***

## My Day!

Ring, ring, ring! The loud noise of the bell echoing in my ear awakens me from slumber. The violators have come to assemble the garbage discarded by those rich, idle people.

I quickly scamper into my hiding place, waiting anxiously until they move on to the next alleyway. Yes, I live in an alleyway. This gloomy and prohibited alleyway is all I've got; however, I appreciate it as I am a street Arab and have no one to share my love with.

I have scant money to purchase breakfast even though I have a job. That's where I'm going next. I know this is wrong but it's my way of survival. Next door is the slaughterhouse. The stale odour of raw, uncooked meat cleaves to me and leaves a putrid smell of dead animal.

I feel a shiver up my back as the hacking of the butcher's knife finally stops stabbing the carcass on the wooden slab. I risk my chances. My heart thudding, fist tightly clenched, head spinning wide-eyed, I run into the shop and purloin a piece of meat. Now I'm late for work. I feel emotionally drained. I run shuddering at the thought of the punishment and consequences if I am late. Nobody enjoys being whipped.

I reach the towering, mystifying building. I feel a dark shadow creep upon me. I stare up into the cold, barbarian eyes of my master. His eyes growing hungry to inflict some more pain, more misery and ruin more lives . . . *help!*

***Kinari Mehta (11)***
***Barham Primary School***

## A Day In The Life Of A Victorian Child

The luminous sun shines brightly on my face. I wake, tired on the hard earth in the street, filled with hustle and bustle of the town people. I rise, knowing I have lived another day in the cruel and unjust world. Oh no, the sun is high in the sky which means I am late for work. My heart thumps hard on my chest, it races with me until I am at work. I pull myself together as I know there will be a punishment waiting for me.

A huge shadow falls on me and his huge body confronts me. The boss takes his never-ending cane out from the leather bag fastened to his leather belt and as fast as lightning, slashes the back of my ripped knees. I take my left hand out, I close my eyes and he slashes again leaving behind a sore bruise tattooed right across my hand. I feel the pain rise in my head and then down to the back of my feet, but I dare not cry as I know if I do, I will get another hit.

Overhearing my boss say 'That boy is useless' the memory of being sold for a pound and ten pence flashes in my head. With tears in my eyes I start my work.

I step into the black hole. My face tears apart as it runs down the rough surface. It gets smothered by the soot and the leftover flesh on my knees rips. I slip, my feet burn as I try stopping myself. I can't, I fall to the bottom and gradually black surrounds me.

***Radhika Kotecha (11)***
***Barham Primary School***

## A Day In The Life Of A Victorian

I was running down a dark gloomy and deserted street. I stopped, I knew that dark building, it was where my parents were killed. I kept on running, I knew that smell, it was the smell of innocent animals being killed. I started to run faster. A feeling came over me like someone had stabbed me. I could see rats running about, I could hear their bare feet on the dark road. I saw the fruit shop with some big, red, juicy apples so I took one when no one was looking. I kept on running, I was ten minutes late. I was running for my life then I tripped over a rat, I was doomed. I could hear children's cries. I looked up into the sky the clouds formed a strange picture of my boss hitting me. I stared at the clouds for a moment and then I heard a crack and I started to sprint. My heart was beating so loud all the rats ran away in terror.

The sky changed from a dark gloomy green to a tulip pink and then it changed again into a sparkling glittering blue with white sequins on it. It was like blue bells ringing. I was admiring the sky but I had to run faster than ever. I knew what was going to happen, I could feel it, hear it, see it and even smell it. Then I got to work and was just about to start when this strange smell and a big dark shadow came behind me with something flexible in his hand. Oh no, *help!*

***Martina O'Donnell (11)***
***Barham Primary School***

## A Day In The Life Of A Victorian

I am woken up by the mine diggers who bang upon a hard old ragged rock. I get up with a struggle as I have been beaten many times by my horrible boss. I live in this alley as my parents abandoned me at a very young age. I have no family, I am a poor, young child begging for a family. As I walk through the darkness of the alleyway, it reminds me of my childhood. As I get to the end I see people elated, jubilant and rapturous at the joy of the market. I quickly run up to the banana stall and sneak two bananas for my breakfast and lunch. The woman does not see me as she has very bad eyesight. I run off in a hurry as I have to go to work in a short time.

When I get to work I head straight up the chimney. As I am climbing I feel a tight pull on my side then I realise I am stuck. I hear my boss taking gigantic steps, thumping on the ground. He starts to tug me and tries to pull me out of the chimney. He grabs me and gives me some good blazing whips. I run off and find myself in the alley and as I close my eyes gently . . .

***Cassandra Linton (11)***
***Barham Primary School***

## A Day In My Life

I woke up one hot morning when the clouds were velvet blue and the sun was as light as a candle lamp. I was only six and three quarters.

I thought about when a nasty old miser named Mr Owli found me coiled up like a snake in the street. He took me straight to his death camp as we call it. He told me to sign a contract which paid me 3p every day but the downfall was you had to wake up at 2am and finish at 10pm.

I started working in the mine. There was a canal going along the top of the mine. Suddenly the water rushed all over my near naked body. I swam (I know how to swim because the rich people threw me into the River Thames). Anyway, I found some steps so I walked to the boss's office. He said 'What are you doing up here?'
'The mine is flooded' I said.
'I do not go and drain the water out so carry on'
So I went down and drained out the mucky water and then I carried on for the next 10 hours. At the end of the day the boss gave me 3p so I went to get a drink that's only 2p. That would buy some lager so I bought it. I knew I should not complain, otherwise I would get sacked so I went back to my disorientated life.

***Aman Abrol (11)***
***Barham Primary School***

## A Day In The Life Of A Victorian Child

I get up and walk to work. I grab a fresh bottle of milk as the cart rushes away. With fear of being punished by the driver, I run away, knowing if I get caught I will be punished severely. Two minutes away from the building, I drink the milk in desperate hungry gulps and enter the building before I get whipped for being late.

I go down a filthy, thin chimney and obliterate the filth, then repeat it eight more times of hard, suffocating work. I go down with my pal Tom and munch dry, crusty bread with half a cup of water. Then I watch Tom getting whipped because Mrs White was not satisfied with her chimney.

The boss gives me twelve more horrifying, dirty chimneys, that happens to destroy me. Then I rush off to Mrs White's and wash her chimney out for her and get 5p extra as a reward. I wipe our eleven more exhausting chimneys which is very tiring, just like every other day. I now go and eat my dinner.

Today I had to have a bowl full of lumpy, tasteless potatoes that went down my dry, sore throat. I go with the boss to inspect the chimney. I know I will be as dead as a zombie if I haven't polished it.

As I go home, I feel blood rushing through me and I lay down on my cardboard box, praying to God that I do not have to live another cruel day on this road.

***Sonkia Rajput (10)***
***Barham Primary School***

## A Day In The Life Of Venus Williams

Every day I rise early - about six o'clock - it's not too early. Sometimes I read the newspaper or I look out of the window and see all the beautiful sights. Then I go for a bath, I make it nice and hot. When I get out of the bath, I get my tennis gear ready and then wake my dad and sister up. While they're getting ready I eat my breakfast. When they're ready, they eat theirs. Once everyone is ready we set off. It is a five minute walk to the training ground, it isn't far. It's a clay court, smaller than the Wimbledon court and it has green fencing all the way around it.

I trained hard, I played my dad and sister several times. Most of the time I won but once or twice I lost against them. 'We train fair, we play fair' we promised each other. Then we went home, ate and had a rest.

My dad told me to get all the tennis gear that we were taking to be repaired so my sister and I had something to play with. Once everything was ready we set off to Wimbledon. We stayed for a long time, about seven to eight hours. It seemed like five minutes. While we waited to play each other, we played against some of the ball boys and girls. They were quite good I must say. They should play for Great Britain. The time roared past, one minute I was teaching, next minute I was walking towards the court to play against my sister.

I saw Dad going to his seat. I watched as everyone else clambered to their seats. Serena walked up to me.
'V - are you okay?'
'Eh . .. hu . . . oh, em yeah I'm fine.'
We started, I served, it was out, a second service. I started again. I threw the ball up and hit it over the net. From then on the rest of the game went smoothly. I won but I was a bit upset that I beat my sister. Serena was upset but I guess it was emotion. We had a celebration. I had a wonderful day.

***Tobi Otudeko (9)***
***Bourne Primary School***

## A Day In The Life Of Queen Elizabeth

Amie woke up on a cold day, not in her own bed, to find she was in the Queen's bedroom. Amie had brown hair, green eyes and white teeth. She had always wanted to be the queen and now she was in the Queen's room. But how did she get there? Nobody knew.

Amie thought about what would happen if someone came in. What would she say? She woke up and was here! Then someone came in and said 'Hello' it was the maid. Amie thought to herself 'Why did she not ask why I was here?'

Amie looked in the mirror to see she looked like the Queen. The maid had black hair, blue eyes and white teeth. She then told Amie that she was going to another country to see some people and that was all for the day.

Amie put on a long dress with rings and earrings. Then she went down to where she was taken by plane. Once she had seen the people, she went back for dinner. When she had finished her dinner, she went to her room and said 'I liked being the Queen but I do not want to be the Queen forever.'

***Leanne Retter (11)***
***Bourne Primary School***

## A Day In The Life Of Britney Spears

A day in the life of Britney Spears would be interesting. With all that money a pop star could really expand her shopping skills (no wonder she looks so nice).

When Britney was born it was thought that she would never reach stardom. Now look at her. She was born in 1980 and her birthday has now come, so Britney has turned twenty.

Britney's songs have always been a big hit except there was one favourite, 'Baby One More Time'. She has released more than five singles, the latest being 'Oops I Did It Again'.

Dinner has now become more posh and more often For Britney Spears. He money has expanded further where dinner is involved. Britney's healthy food and lovely restaurant must have paid off.

Pop stars have always been my favourite people, this is what I think. I would love to go out to dinner with friends or pop bands or singers, especially Artful Dodger or Rich out of Five.

***Toni Phillips (11)***
***Bourne Primary School***

## A DAY IN THE LIFE OF DAVID BECKHAM

I woke up at 7:00am to check on my wife and baby, then I got dressed, watched TV and ate my breakfast.

By 9:30am I went out for some football training with some of my friends, while my wife and baby went out to do some shopping. When they came back at 10:30am she showed me a ring that she had bought me that said 'I love you'.

At lunchtime we went to a big and fancy restaurant to eat.

At 4:00pm I had to go and play a football match with some of my friends, against Newcastle. Unfortunately they lost 1-0. My wife was very proud of me as she came to cheer for our team.

In the evening my wife and I decided to go and buy an expensive car, a very big one. When we came back, Brooklyn was fast asleep so we put him to bed while we ate our dinner and watched TV. Then we went to bed.

Goodnight.

***Anita Rajani (11)***
***Bourne Primary School***

## A Day In The Life Of My Mum

*Monday morning:*
My mum gets up early and does my breakfast and then my cousin comes as my mum looks after him. Then she takes me half way to school. Then she does different jobs around the house or she goes to Ruislip or Uxbridge. My mum then waits for a little girl called Lily to come and look after her.

*Monday afternoon:*
My mum gives Lily and Ashley their lunch, then she takes Ashley to nursery and Lily has a sleep. My nan looks after Lily while she is asleep so Mum can go swimming. After swimming, Mum picks me up from school and she still has Lily.

*Monday evening:*
Mum cooks our dinner and after, gives Lily a bath. Then Lily goes home and Mum sometimes plays a game with us.

***Samantha Pegram (9)***
***Bourne Primary School***

## My Mum At Work

My mum, Lisa, is a policewoman based at Uxbridge Police Station. Below, I have shown a typical night duty shift for her. I hope you enjoy it.

*Evening*
Mum has a bath and gets ready for work. At 9pm she leaves for work, arriving about five minutes later.

*10pm*
At 10pm, Mum and her friends are sitting on parade, listening to who is wanted and having a much-needed cup of tea.

*2am*
Mum has been driving around with another PC dealing with calls. She has reported a burglary, split up a fight, dealt with a domestic disturbance and now it is time for her to have something to eat!

*6am*
At 6am Mum arrives home. She walks Jasper, the dog, makes my lunch for school, lays out my uniform, gets my breakfast and then sits down for a cup of tea.

*7:30am*
Whilst I am having breakfast, Mum is getting ready for bed. She is looking forward to a nice, long sleep!

***Jack Stevenson (9)***
***Bourne Primary School***

## THE LIFE OF JAMES BOND

I would like to be James Bond because you can shoot everyone and fight everyone.

One day, Q gave me a car with rockets that come out of the sun roof and lasers that come out of the wheels to burst their wheels, and a lady voice-navigator.

Bond jumps into the car and into action! I went to the top of England where the Russians were attacking. I parked in a car park. I stayed in the car, the rockets were shot and a couple of Russians were dead. The Russians attacked my wheels and tried to burst my tyres. I shot them with my lasers and I killed a few people.

I went back to Q and said 'I've located the Russian base.'
'Good, now you can go back to blow it up. Take this plane.'
I flew it to the base and put loads of bombs on the base and blew them up. All the Russians were dead. I flew back to Q. I knew I had completed the mission. When I got back, Q said 'You've completed the mission.'

***Sam Wilson (9)***
***Bourne Primary School***

## A Day In The Life Of Rachel From S Club 7

Rachel got up, she got washed and dressed, she had breakfast and got in the car. The driver drove her to her friend's house. First she arrived at Hannah's house and Tina was there with her. They both jumped in and they all zoomed away in the car. The next stop they made was Bradley's house. Bradley was waiting outside. He ran and jumped into the car and once again they zoomed off. After they picked Bradley up, they picked up Jo, Paul and Jon. They all had something to eat. They were in a rush because the seven of them had a gig to go to at the Party In The Park. They were a little late, but on the way there was traffic.
'Oh no!' said Bradley.
'What should we do now?' said Tina
'There is nothing to do but just wait here,' said Paul.
No one was behind them.
'I have an idea!' said the driver. 'I have a police siren.'
'Great idea!' Jo shouted out. The driver reached over to his glove compartment and took the siren and put it on the top of the car. Away they went. Finally they got to the gig and sang their hearts out.

***Rochelle Donaldson (9)***
***Bourne Primary School***

## A Day In The Life Of David Beckham

I woke up early, at about 6:00am, I put some clothes on and went downstairs. I turned on the hob and put the frying pan on it, then I took some rashers of bacon out of the fridge and laid some in the pan. Then I got a packet of six eggs out of the fridge. I put a saucer on the grill, warmed it up and put the eggs in. About half an hour later, I put the bacon and eggs on a plate, got a knife and fork out of the drawer. Then I took the plate into the dining room. I put the TV on and started to watch the news while I was eating.

Twenty minutes later, I put my shoes on and walked to the local newsagent's. When I got to the newsagent's, I picked up a Sun, gave the shopkeeper 30p and took the newspaper home. When I got home, I went upstairs and put my England tracksuit training kit on. Then I went back downstairs, put my boots in a carrier bag and put my trainers on. I went outside and locked the door. I walked round to my shiny, red Jaguar. I unlocked the door and sat on the sea. I started the engine and I started my journey to Wembley.

After an hour, I finally arrived at Wembley. I took my boots to the pitch and then put them on. I got a ball and then started to kick it around with Paul Scholes and Alan Shearer. Then I started to do some stretches and running across the pitch. Then Keegan and the other players arrived at the stadium. Keegan put out some cones for the players to dribble around.

Half an hour later, Keegan tells me to go and give Seaman, Martyn and Wright some shots. I walked over to the goal with the three goalies and I started to take some shots.

Forty-five minutes later, Keegan told me to come back with the three keepers. I walked back with the goalkeepers, then the whole squad started to do some short passes. Then they did some longer passes, and then we did some passes right across the pitch.

At 4:00pm they all finished. I put my trainers back on and then I went in my red Jaguar and drove back to Manchester. On the way home, I had to get some petrol, get some food from the supermarket and get some money from the bank to pay for the petrol and the food. By the time I arrived at the bank it was already 5:00pm. I popped into the bank to get some money, then I went to the supermarket, then I got some petrol and then drove home.

When I got home, it was 5:45pm, so I put on some chips and fish fingers. When they were ready, I sat down at the table and watched TV. When I had finished my meal, I put the plate in the sink and watched a bit of TV. Then at 9:00pm I went to bed.

***Ian O'Connell (9)***
***Bourne Primary School***

## A Day In The Life Of Jo From S Club 7

Jo got up out of her warm bed. Jo was still tired, so she had a bath. The bath was warm like her bed, it woke her up. Jo got dressed and had breakfast. She brushed her teeth and hair. By the time she got out of the door, it was 10 o'clock, the limo was waiting. In the limo it was a bit hot, but Jo could not open the window in case someone saw her. She picked up the rest of the band to rehearse the TV programme. After they had lunch with the manager. Jo left the rest of the band and went to the city for an interview. The limo took Jo to see the new film called 'Chicken Run', it was about two hours before she had dinner. After dinner, she went back to the hotel and she went to bed. Sweet dreams.

***Zoë Long***
***Bourne Primary School***

## A Day In The Life Of Olivia

Olivia wakes up at 6am, has a feed and gets dressed by Mummy and walks me to school.

Mummy comes home at 12pm and picks me up from school at 3pm and Olivia has a feed and a nappy change and things like that.

In the evening, Olivia has baby food and Mummy puts her into her pyjamas and rocks her to sleep. I go to bed at 8pm or 8:30pm and Olivia goes to bed at 9pm or 9:30pm.

***Rebecca Barrowman (8)***
***Bourne Primary School***

## The Life Of A Mum

In the morning, she gets her children their breakfast, then she helps them get ready for school. Finally, she gets them into school, then by the time she gets to work, she is an hour late. She has a bad day at work, then she has to go and pick her children up from school. After getting them home and feeding them, she gets them to bed. Their dad walks in from work feeling very hungry. 'What's for tea?' Finally, Mum gets to have a nice rest, but in the morning it starts all over again.

***Samantha Rosario (9)***
***Bourne Primary School***

## A Day In The Life Of My Fantastic Holiday In Florida

15th October 1999
Tomorrow is the big day for us. It's a holiday to Florida, but at a ridiculous time, at 5:00am, so we have to wake up at 3:30am because we have to check that we've got everything.

16th October 1999
'Mum, I don't want to get up,' I said.
'Wake up, we've got a plane to catch!'
When Mum said that, I woke up so quickly. I forgot to put my slippers on. I was so nervous that something might go wrong. I brushed my teeth quickly, but properly. My Grandma and Grandad came to the house to take us to Gatwick Airport. At last we were there! We went to the check-in to check our passports, they were fine, so we went to the waiting room to be called for our flight. 'Please can the people going to Florida please go to the aeroplane desk.' So we went and they checked our pictures in our passports, they were correct, so we all went onto the tube to catch the plane. Then we went onto the plane, we got the numbers of our seats and sat down on them. We heard a voice from the speaker saying 'Please can you get your seat belts on because the plane is taking off.' We put on our seat belts and the plane took off.

It was breakfast time and we had a cereal of our choice. It was terrible. Then I was bored, so I watched TV. Dr Dolittle was on so I watched it.

***Sukhina Sidhu (10)***
***Bourne Primary School***

## A DAY IN THE LIFE OF A WORM

It was a sunny day and I was eating my breakfast - thick, smooth, mud. I'm Wizzy the worm. I live in the garden of George's house. It's good in the summer, we can play in the mud by the paddling pool. It's good when it's been a boiling, sweating, hot day, it will cool us down.

'Come on, let's go and make a hideout down by the hard mud,' said Peter.
'OK, sure we can go down the soft mud and go across.' I said.
'What are we waiting for? Let's go.'
'Oh no, can you hear that? What is it?'
'I don't know.'
'Let's run, go, go, go, run. The spade,' said Peter.
'Stop,' I said, 'you have a brother.'
'What?' Peter said.
'You have a brother,' I gasped again. 'Go straight up to the high ground.'
'Watch out, a bird!' I jumped into some mud. His brother died. 'Help please, he's dead.'
'Watch out,' Peter said to me, 'I was a bird's lunch.'

***Alex Ormrod (10)***
***Bourne Primary School***

## A Day In The Life Of Leanne

As Leanne grew up, she became better and better at art. Her mum, Jo, was a tattooist and when she wanted some tracing done, she asked Leanne to do it because she was so good. One day she went to art class and did a water painting. From that day onwards, she has shown it to everyone, even her mum's customers. After that, she hardly did any art, she kept doing dancing and stuff.

Then one day, she noticed that she hadn't done art for ages and ages, so she tried doing it, but she thought it was strange because she couldn't even draw properly anymore! She just said to herself, 'It's not worth it, I might as well go back to dancing.' So she did. After a couple of months, she was really good at dancing, but then she got really bored with dancing. Then she saw a sign, it had on it 'Need more girl players' so she went in for that. Her mum came to one of the football matches and they won 13-6. Leanne scored eight goals and her mum was really proud.

When her mum had a job coming in, Leanne wanted to do the tracing, but it went all over the place and she was not pleased with herself. So Leanne said to her mum Jo, 'I should have stuck to art.' After a couple of days, Leanne got back to her old self.

***Leanne Phillips (10)***
***Bourne Primary School***

## A Day In The Life Of An FBI Agent

The day started off like any other, having a morning cup of tea with the alien, Zorik. Then the commanding officer came over to me, he gave me the task of capturing Zinka, the fifteen-eyed, fifteen-toed alien who had just gone missing from HQ. My first trip took me to area 51, its position is classified. Then my expedition took me to Seattle where he had been spotted buying a burger at Burger King. There he was, I'd spotted him, now I had him on the run. Just as soon as I'd located him, he vanished around a corner on Fifth Avenue. Then I went to HQ.

I arrived just as he was being locked up in a high security vault underground. My next assignment was to investigate the scene of a sighting of a vanishing multicoloured car and a bright light. From the signs on the road, I knew just who it was! And he was locked up in an FBI vault.

He was very sorry and promised he would not do it again, so another glorious day ended.

***Ben Rosendale (9)***
***Bourne Primary School***

## A Day In The Life Of A Pilot

Dear Diary,

Today I was knighted by the Queen for serving our country in the Second World War.

I was extremely nervous. Butterflies flew around my tummy like a cat after a bird. My family were proud of me and wished me good luck. (I needed it,) I really did hope I wouldn't fall over or say something about those funny hats she wears, the size of Washington DC. I have never really won anything before in my life. I never dreamed of being knighted. With my £100 suit on, I drove in the car to the ceremony. To my left were rows of people, to my right were even more. Although there were loads of people, we were led up to the Queen one by one. Finally, it was my turn. In a very high-pitched voice she said 'How very nice to meet you, Sir.' She was wearing a funny hat but I said nothing. She lifted a box and gave it to my shaking hand. I knelt down on one knee. She lifted her sword onto my shoulder and said her bit. The crowd roared, cheered and clapped. I shook her hand, turned around and gave a bow.

I never expected anything like this. I will always remember this day as long as I live. Nothing could ever beat this, I will always wear my medal. I get stopped on the streets. I knew how nervous I could be, but everything went well.

***Victoria Leahy (10)***
***Bourne Primary School***

## A Day In The Life Of Alan Shearer

My name is Alan Shearer and today is June 17th 2000. We are playing Germany tonight and it is one of the most important games of my career.

My alarm clock had woken me, but not Tony. I couldn't help feeling sorry for him because he really wanted to play, but he's injured.

I went to the living room where Robbie and Michael were sharing a joke. All the lads were nervous, you could tell because no one spoke about the game. After breakfast, I read the newspaper, the press have criticised me a lot lately but tonight I will prove myself. Later, I went to the relaxation room where the Nevilles were playing pool and Dennis was playing cards and winning by the look of his smile. In the corner, Tony was reading Shakespeare. David was phoning Victoria to check on Brooklyn. Later we headed for the coach. Just before I left, I saw a picture of my three girls, I will win this match for them.

When we arrived, we warmed up on the pitch. The time was 8:40pm, the stadium, Charleroi. In the tunnel I looked back and out of the red shirts, I saw the familiar sight of Ince's bare chest. We walked out of the tunnel and the crowd roared, the noise was so loud. We sang the national anthem, I was so proud.

Michael and I stepped up to take the kick-off, the whistle went, it had begun . . .

***Nick Glenday (10)***
***Bourne Primary School***

## A Day In The Life Of Danielle And Simone At Chessington

One day last summer, my sister Danielle and I had a fun day at Chessington. To me, it was the best day of the summer holidays. even better than the week we spent at Bournemouth. When we arrived at Chessington, Danielle went to get the tickets. When we got in, there were loads of rides surrounding us. I didn't know which ride to go on first. Danielle went on the first ride, which was called Rameses' Revenge, it was too scary for me. The next ride we went on together was called the Vampire. My favourite ride of all was the Bubble Works. It was so good that I went on it another two times. Danielle's favourite ride was the Logger's Leap. To get on the rides, we had to queue up for quite a long time. For lunch, we had a picnic that my mum made for us, so we ate it sitting on the grass. After we had eaten our lunch, Danielle bought me an ice-lolly, and we bought some gifts from the shop. Danielle decided we could go on some more rides. My aunt and uncle took us home at about 8pm. We had been at Chessington since 10am, so we had a really long day out which Danielle and I really enjoyed. For our next trip, Danielle and I want to go to Thorpe Park.

***Simone Monks (10)***
***Bourne Primary School***

## A Day In The Life Of Neil Armstrong

Today, John F Kennedy's wish had come true. The first man's landed on the moon. Neil Armstrong and two other people called Buzz Aldrin and Michael Collins. Neil Armstrong was 38, the oldest. Buzz Aldrin was 35 years old and the youngest, Michael Collins, was 34. They all were married.

Neil Armstrong was first to come out, followed by Buzz Aldrin and Michael Collins had to stay inside to take care of the spacecraft. When Neil Armstrong first landed on the moon, he spoke this famous quote: 'The Eagle has landed. One small step for man, and a giant leap for mankind.'

They named their rocket Apollo 11. It had thirty-two floors. They lived on the highest floor, called Columbia. They needed sleeping bags attached to the ground because they had less gravity, or they would be flying in the air! In the rocket, their living style was really different. They had to eat cubes of bacon with tea. Yuck! To check the gravity, Neil Armstrong tried dropping a spoon, but it stayed in the air!

On the twenty-first of July, Apollo 11 had landed. On the moon, Neil Armstrong and Buzz Aldrin discovered lots of things. Before they left the moon, Neil Armstrong left the American flag, and it's still there!

And that was a day in the life of Neil Armstrong!

***Arushi Gandhi (9)***
***Bourne Primary School***

## A Day In The Life Of Misty

My name is Misty. I am a completely black cat, well almost, apart from a white spot on my chest. At the moment, I am in an adoption centre in London.
'Hello,' said a voice. I turned round and looked, it was a human. I walked cautiously towards her. I thought that nobody would want me because I am pregnant with kittens.
'Come on, I won't hurt you,' whispered the voice. I let her stroke me. The man from the adoption centre asked her if she wanted to take me home.
'Yes please,' she said. Within an hour, they were trying to get me in a cat basket. I wasn't going to go without a fair fight, so I miaowed and miaowed, but to them it seemed insignificant. Finally I gave up and got in. It was a long way to my new home. I had been in the car for over twenty minutes and my stomach was aching. I knew what was happening and I knew I didn't have much time.

As soon as we arrived at the house, I scurried up the stairs to find a place to rest. I searched until I found a towel and lay down. I realised my kittens were coming. The first tiny kitten was black, this was followed by a white one and then a third came, a little black and white one.

What a lovely day. First a beautiful new home and now I am a mother.

***Mark Grimes (10)***
***Bourne Primary School***

## A Day In The Life Of A Pike

Lurk in reeds patiently for an oblivious dace, perch or pike to drift by to be a perfect meal.

Retreat back to thick undergrowth of algae and weeds, ever alert for meals and avoid fishermen's bits of wood and plastic with hooks. Fish swiftly speed by and I hurtle at top speed as it desperately tries everything possible to evade me. As I catch it up, it tires but still ducks and dives and manoeuvres away. Still I keep moving and it speeds on until one mighty swish from my tail propels me alongside my victim and the chase is brought to an end by the perch evading my bite and escaping. So I retreat to my weedy array of camouflage and wait silently for another fish to swim past.

Another fish dumbly swims past and I speed forwards. To my horror it was a hook and I have been deceived. As it is jerked further up into my lip. I struggle and strain and twist as I am reeled in closer to the fisherman. I am tiring out rapidly and eventually, just give up until I am at the surface. Then I make one valiant dive down to the depths and suddenly to my luck, the hook slid out gently. It was a barbless hook. I was safe. A few minutes later, the same sort of lure came down again and I avoided it fully.

I am never guaranteed to even chase prey, but sooner or later, one swishes by and the chase is on.

***Alex Philpott (10)***
***Bourne Primary School***

## A Day In The Life Of Tim Henman

It should have been a normal day for Tim Henman, the British No.1. 3rd July 2000 was when Mark Philipoussis of Australia took on British Tim Henman and the Aussie beat the British three sets to two. The sets were 6-1 to Mark, 5-7 Tim, 6-7 Tim, 6-3 Mark and 6-4 Mark. British and Australian fans of the two players were sitting on the edge of their seats and British fans were especially cheering to keep Britain in the Wimbledon Tournament of 2000. Luckily, he went 2-1 up in sets, but then his opponent, Philipoussis equalled that to 2-2 in sets. Then the last set was crucial. Who was going to win?

The last games went 1-0, 2-0, 2-1, 2-2, 3-2, 4-2, 4-3, 5-3, 5-4. Now if Tim won this set, he could have won Wimbledon 2000, but Mark Philipoussis won that game, which gave the whole match a wrap and he started to let the Australian flag fly high as our Union Jack gets taken right down and we are all out. All British fans of tennis are now all waving goodbye as we are knocked out, but Australian fans must be waving hello to the quarter-finals, as Philipoussis swims through with no problems at all. Goodbye Tim Henman. Hello Philipoussis, look forward to the quarter-finals. The last set and game is what Henman really wanted to win. All that mattered was Henman had to win the last set, but unluckily he lost and Australian win might be just around the corner, beckoning for Philipoussis to come closer and win in the finals.

***Andrew Nisbet (10)***
***Bourne Primary School***

## A Day In The Life Of A Dinosaur

Hi, my name is Clippo and I am a Tyrannosaurus Rex. I am a dinosaur that eats meat, which unfortunately means I eat other dinosaurs.

I don't have a mum or dad as they both died when I was only young. I don't have many friends either, which is quite sad, but I still enjoy myself wandering around the forest and eating when I'm hungry. Any way, this is the story of how my life and the life of all my ancestors finally ended.

I woke up this morning to a very hot, sticky day and to a sound that I had never heard before. I ran over to the edge of the mountain to see if I could see what was happening. As I started to run, I felt the earth tremble beneath me. I ran down the hill calling out to the others, trying to find out what was going on. As I reached the bottom, I could see a big hole at least three miles wide and as long as my eyes could see. Inside the hole were thousands of dinosaurs and the ground was moving all around them. I tried to reach some of them but they were too far down. All of a sudden, there was an enormous bang and fire was pouring down the side of the mountain.

I was so scared I didn't know what to do, so I started running as fast as I could. As I looked behind me, I could see other dinosaurs running behind me. Then the earth started moving again and big holes were opening up in front of me, I kept running, jumping and leaping as hard as I could until eventually I reached the other side of the hill.

I stopped to catch my breath and as I turned around I could see the fire everywhere, the earth was crumbling and mile long crack were appearing everywhere. I was so frightened I didn't know what to do. I decided my only chance would be to make a run for the other side of the mountain. I called to a few dinosaurs that were at my side and beckoned them to follow me. There was another tremble this time, bigger than the others, so I took off up the side of the mountain as quickly as I could. By now I was aching. My whole body shaking with fear and tiredness.

The next and last thing I remember was an enormous explosion and I fell down a huge hole in the ground. Was this it, is this the end of the dinosaurs? Is this the end of the world?

Only you know the answer to that now!

***Zara Nogales (10)***
***Bourne Primary School***

## A Day In The Life Of My Mum

My mum was born approximately 30 years before me. I was born in 1990.

My grandmother had five children including my mum. In Barbados, times were hard. Then, they didn't earn a lot of money. In 1980, the family moved from Barbados to England, my mum was then 15 years old. They moved to West Ealing. Mum went to St Ann's Secondary Girls' School in Hanwell.

At 16, she left school and went to Southall Further Education College and studied for her O-Level examinations. She also did a Pre-Nursing course. When Mum finished college, she got a job in East London opposite All Saints Church, Isle of Dogs. It was very expensive for Mum to go to work. She spent £10 getting there, £12 travelling to the patients' houses and £10 getting home. Altogether, it cost her £160 a week. She thought this was ridiculous, so she changed her place of work to Ealing. This journey is short and it costs less.

My mum is planning to return to Barbados for good. This is not good. At Barbados it is rubbish. It is hardly exciting and I don't want to move.

Our favourite day together was one day last month, when we went to Buckingham Palace. We spent the whole day together, having lots of fun and laughter.

***Monique Belgrave (9)***
***Bourne Primary School***

## A Day In The Life Of Neil Armstrong

Today was the day that Neil Armstrong and his two partners were going on an extraordinary journey into space, where nobody had ever been before . . . it was to the moon.

Scientists had invented a space rocket that would take Neil Armstrong and his two partners to the moon. They had to wear protective suits and helmets so they could breathe oxygen from the tanks which were strapped at the back of their spacesuits.

It was a few more hours until they were going to the moon. Neil Armstrong said goodbye to his family and the crowd were cheering for them. It was time to leave. The three brave men climbed into the space rocket and the countdown started.

Five, four, three, two, one, blast-off!

The rocket took off with a puff of smoke and flames coming out of the pipes. The rocket began to move up, up into the air. Neil Armstrong and his two partners sat on, looking slightly tense. They were flying further away. Soon they had reached the moon. The space rocket landed. The first words Neil Armstrong said were 'The eagle has landed. 'Neil went out first, he was overwhelmed to touch the ground. He got out from the rocket and said 'One step for man, one giant leap for mankind.'

Once they had looked around, they brought an American flag to mark that they had succeeded in their mission. Since then, they have become heroes.

***Cristina Di Genua (9)***
***Bourne Primary School***

## A Day In The Life Of My Dad, A Driving Instructor

In the morning, I would wake up and have my breakfast. Then I would drop my kids off at school. Then I would go and pick up the customer.

Today is a new customer. I will have to go over the basics, which is a controls lesson. All lessons last for an hour and afterwards, I take the customer back to his or her house. Then I go to get the next customer. She is going to have her test today. First I go through all the techniques, then it is her test. Sadly, she doesn't pass. Now it's time for lunch. I make some lunch and watch TV for half an hour, then I walk the dog for ten minutes. Then I go and get the next customer. This lesson is a motorway lesson. Most motorway lessons last about two hours, this is because we have to do a lot of miles. They practice leaving and rejoining the motorway. They practice overtaking and changing lanes. They drive a lot faster on the motorway, up to a maximum of seventy miles per hour. The last lesson of the day is a two hour lesson for a boy who's got his test in a week's time. He wants two hours because he needs to practice his reverse parking and his reversing around the corner. He also wants to practice lots of roundabouts.

After this, I drive myself home, park the car and have a beer to relax after a stressful day.

***Joe Bridle (10)***
***Bourne Primary School***

## A Day In The Life Of My Brother Josh

Josh wakes up about 6.45 he always calls my name to see if I'm awake.

We come downstairs for breakfast and we watch TV together till it's time to get ready for school. Just before we leave for school Josh always picks a car to play with in the playground. When the whistle goes he looks for me to give me a kiss goodbye and always waves at me, and off he goes home with mum. So while I'm at school, Josh likes to help mum with her jobs at home because tonight after school there's a family barbecue in the school playground.

Josh is looking forward to going on the bouncy castle. We get home from school and get ready, but just before we leave Josh and I played football out in the garden, because he loves to play football. Then he fell down the steps and started to cry because when I looked, he had a big cut on his leg. I called for our mum to come and collect Josh to clean up his leg and after that it was time to go to the barbecue.

Josh was a bit shy to start off with because he had to get used to all the people around him - which didn't take very long. We had our burgers and hot-dogs, then Josh and my friends went on the bouncy castle. My friends all made a fuss of him, perhaps because he's so cute!

Next we're all off to the disco, and all my friends wanted to dance with him. It's time for the barbecue to end and we say goodbye to everyone.

Josh has had such a good time that we don't think he'll be able to walk home, so dad had to carry him. He put his thumb in his mouth and after five minutes he was fast asleep - he is only three.

***Charlotte Moorse (10)***
***Bourne Primary School***

## A Day In The Life Of A Sniper

My mission was to eliminate any German troops within the code-named town of Cosvant, so that the British troops could move forward to make an assault on the next town.

Once we had reached Cosvant, I had some cover fire, so I could find a place to hide. I chose to hide, and set up behind a wall with a few holes in it. One of the holes was big enough to fit the end of my sniper rifle through. I was well equipped with over 200 sniper bullets and over 1000 M16 bullets.

When the enemy was within target range, I fired at the end trooper. The enemy had obviously realised that there was a sniper firing at them, but they didn't know from where, so one by one I killed them.

A keypoint of being a sniper is to never have any mercy for the enemy, but I still didn't believe in murder.

British troops moved cautiously through the town, but didn't spot the German sniper who killed two men. Once I realised where the sniper was I knew I had to move forward because he wasn't within my firing range, I heard someone coming up the stairs, I fired, it was Thomas a British trooper.

I was aghast and eliminated the sniper quickly, so that I can build and dig a grave for my dead friend.

My mission was complete.

***Sean McShane (11)***
***Bourne Primary School***

## A Day In The Life Of Courtney Cox

If I was Courtney Cox I would have very busy days. I would have to wake up really early to get to work. My work would be long and tiring, just to make one episode. As well as being hard work, it would also be five hours of excitement.

After work I would go home and phone some of my friends, for instance: Jennifer Aniston or Lisa Kudrow and we would go on a massive shopping spree. Going into all the famous shops and spending way too much money on things we don't need. This shopping would take up the majority of the day, but once it was over I would go home, see my husband and watch a few films before I went to bed. I would go to bed quite early because I was so tired.

Then I would wake up and it would all start again and all day I could enjoy myself again.

***Kathleen Gray (11)***
***Bourne Primary School***

## A Day In The Life Of Bruce Willis

I woke up very early so we could shoot the new film. I raced down the road in my Porsche and I was excited because really I didn't know what it was called.

After shooting the film I took sixty grand out of the bank and bought a brand new Bentley (so now in total I have seven cars). I washed and admired the car for five minutes then I drove down to the beach with the family.

Everyone would ask me if I was Bruce Willis and I would say 'No, I don't know who you're talking about!'

Most of the days I try to live a normal life but when you are a film star, you can be quite busy. So at night I look after the family and just watch TV. But there are the odd nights I would be working or I would go out for dinner with my family.

***Karl Graves (11)***
***Bourne Primary School***

## A Day In The Life Of Dennis Wise

I woke up this morning, my butler Thomas made the full English breakfast. After breakfast I ran to the bathroom and got washed. We had to be at training for ten o'clock. So I left at 9.15am, I could take either the Mercedes, the BMW or the Ferrari, in the end I chose the Ferrari. Training went on for three hours, I didn't get back till two o'clock.
I had to get washed again because my wife and my son Henry were going shopping.

We went to Harrods and I bought Henry a huge teddy bear, and I bought a new caravan and boat at Lesley's hi-tech shop. At 6 o'clock I went back to my house and got changed for dinner. I was going to a fancy restaurant called 'Chasbounet' with my wife. It was a French restaurant. The nanny was looking after Henry and we left the restaurant at half nine and we didn't get back till half past ten. Henry was put to bed at nine and we went to bed at eleven o'clock.

***Sam Richardson (11)***
***Bourne Primary School***

## A Day In The Life Of Billie Piper

6.30am My alarm clock goes off at 6.30am and I slowly prise myself out of my comfortable bed and crawl into my clothes. I am still exhausted from the day before (I got to bed at 3am). The car horn sounds and I run down the stairs, slip my shoes on and rush out of the door and jump into the car.

7.00am There is a massive traffic jam and I am running late for a rehearsal for my new video. I eat in the limousine and soon arrive at the gigantic building, in which I am shooting my video. I am feeling nervous.

8.00am I spring into the building and I meet all the people helping with the video. One woman drags me into a room and starts piling all my make-up on. Another woman calls me and starts showing me different clothes for me to wear. I soon chose a Union Jack sparkly top and a pair of old looking jeans.

8.35am A tall man begins talking to me about my dance routine and where it will be shot. I feel excited, but tired.

9.30am We start to film. It is going alright until suddenly two of the camera-men crash into each other. Ahhhgg!

12.30pm

I feel totally bored, the cameras have been sorted and so have the men, therefore I can start filming again.

5.00pm Eventually the producer says it's okay and I can go home. I feel exhausted and want to run to bed, until I remember I have a film premier to go to and then a large party to go to. Oh no!

7.00pm I enter the large building, rush to my seat and begin watching the film. It is really disappointing, but it's okay. I thought it would be more exciting.

9.00pm I am now ready to go to the party, I have had my make-up done, my new clothes on, my hair done and also my nails all costing a total of one thousand pounds - not bad!

10.00pm

I have arrived and feel really tired, but I manage to stay up until 3.30am. I get home by taxi and get changed and go to my comfy bed only thinking of tomorrow. Waking up at 6.30am again, going to bed at 3.am again - just another day for me.

***Hannah Constable (11)***
***Bourne Primary School***

## A Day In The Life Of Lisa Kudrow From Friends (Phoebe)

*How the day begins*

I have to wake up at five in the morning and be at the studios in New York at seven in the morning. I normally arrive when David Ross and Courtney (Monica) are there, the others arrive shortly after me once everyone has arrived and we start straight away on the scenes.

*The Scenes*

My favourite part of the day is when you find out what scenes you're in. Matt (Joey) and I like to share each others' scripts as we find it the hardest to act the thick ones. Phoebe isn't thicker than Joey but mostly can come out with the silly things. Everyone knows that Phoebe has always had a soft spot for Joey but some day, I think there will be a scene when Joe and Phoebe get together.

*Clothes*

I don't really like some of the clothes I wear nor do the others, whatever kinds of clothes you get, you have got to wear them, whether they make you look fat or kind of tarty.

*What I think of Phoebe*

Phoebe is a fun person to play, sometimes I wish I didn't have to work every day because working ten hours a day and you only get an hour break - is a lot of work. I have to eat very healthy food as I have to have a good figure to play Phoebe.

*Being in 'Friends'*

Being in Friends is like a dream come true. I get along with the rest of the cast just as if we've been friends all along and it's fun to know that we have fans all over the world, who enjoy the programme.

***Sophie Kimmins (11)***
***Bourne Primary School***

## A Day In The Life Of Lita

I get up at 7.15am and have my 85% fat-free breakfast. Then I see what's happening on the Wrestling Month, week and day table. I meet up with the Hardy Boyz to go swimming and to work out. When I need a vacation I go down to my villa in Miami.

Matt and Jeff are my two best friends. Whenever T and A attack me Matt and Jeff use there daredevil stunts to save me. Ever since I have been with them I have learnt new moves and been able to beat people.

On my holidays there are so many things to do. When I'm on the beach I usually go surfing and jet-skiing. When I jet-ski the best bits are jumping over waves and diving under them.

The best shops I know are in New York. There are many shops, but Tiffany's is the best of the best.

***Scott Roberts (11)***
***Bourne Primary School***

## A DAY IN THE LIFE OF CLERGY BRIAN REED

*Sundays*

8.15am Brian wakes up and prays before getting dressed. He then checks his Church diary to see what he has got to do that day. Then he eats his breakfast, not forgetting to pray afterwards.

9.30am Brian drives to church for his Daily Communion and Service. As clergy, Brian must be in robes for the service, a cassock and a surplice.

10.45am

Brian gets changed and goes to the Thompson Room (Vestry) to put away the bread, wine and cutlery.

11.00am

Brian walks to the Church Hall and has refreshments. After which he helps clean up as the church choirboys: Mark Hurst, Chris Girdlestone and Sam Spettigue ring the bells for the next service.

11.50am

The next service is Pentecost and a feast of mashed potatoes, meat and coca cola is had at the Church Hall.

1.30pm Brian goes home for an afternoon nap and for lunch.

4.00pm Brian drives to the Rectory where Rev Phillip lives to get ready for the Confirmation Class.

5.00pm The Confirmation Class arrives; Sam Spettigue, Mark, Ellie Chris and Lucy Bradbury are in the class.

7.00pm The class finishes and the pupils go home. Brian goes home to pray.

9.00pm Brian watches Emmerdale and goes to bed.

9.30pm Brian's day has ended.

***Samuel Spettigue (11)***
***Bourne Primary School***

## A Day In The Life Of My Cat

I am a cat and my name is Spike.

My fur is black but when I sit in the sun it looks brown. In the morning when I wake up from sleeping under Grace's bunkbed, I come downstairs and purr as loud as I can to let Grace know that I'm hungry and I would like my breakfast. I usually get Whiskas.

Grace's mum and dad have made life hard for me by putting wooden flooring down and when I try to creep in at night to sleep under Grace's bed, they can now hear me and try to chase me out again. But Grace sneaks back downstairs and lets me in. Some things will never change.

By Spike Hennessy.

***Grace Hennessy (9)***
***Bourne Primary School***

## THE DAY IN THE LIFE OF MY DAD

One morning my dad work up extra early to get up to Barnes where he works. He works for Wallgame Limited, so then he dropped me off at my school, Bourne Primary. My dad's job is to make picture frames.

The traffic was very bad and my dad was trying and trying, but he still couldn't get out of the traffic. Suddenly he rushed through, and got to work although it was a bit of a job.

At work there were some customers and he sorted them out and they got what they wanted. My dad heard something crackling and pushing, water droplets came out of the wall, slowly near the kitchen where he was making tea. Then the day was sunny again and gradually warm and hot so the massive puddle-like flood dried up. My dad was relieved, although there were a few wet patches left - but not much.

Ding! Ding! Ding! Went the door as my dad's friends came in
'Hi Paul!' shouted my dad.
'All right Rob?'
'You got a puncture!'
'Really, let's get a new tyre!'
So that's what they did.
'Oh no!' yelled my dad
'What, what is it?'
'My keys, they're in the car.'

So then Paul realised that the car window was open slightly and my dad got hold of a stick with a hook on and got the spare keys out of the container. Then very carefully we wiggled the key through the skimpy window.

***Sophie Dalmedo (9)***
***Bourne Primary School***

## A DAY IN THE LIFE OF A TEACHER

6.00am. The alarm clock shrieks in my ear, I pull my cosy, warm quilt over my head. A few minutes later I stomp out of bed, then stomp down the stairs.

I'm downstairs and I get my Weetabix . . . 'Mmmm' lovely warm milk warming up my tummy, the Weetabix swishing around my mouth. Time to have a lovely hot cup of tea. Tea's made and I swallow my tea.

I've woken up a bit, but I'm still sleepy.

I zoomed up the stairs into the bathroom - running late.
I saw my hair . . . It was outrageous. It was all topsy-turvy.
I scrubbed and scrubbed my teeth, washed my face until it was red.
I've finished washing and I put on my clothes: blue blouse and trousers my hair looks much better now.

It was time to go to work 'Oh no!' I was in my classroom. As I was approaching my class the noise was getting louder and louder. I arrived at my classroom and I screamed, I was horrified by the level of noise, they became quieter.

I kept getting everything wrong, I couldn't concentrate. Everyone was laughing at me, I felt stupid - I was red.

I couldn't even do my 4s, 10s, 9s and 2s - it was hilarious.

The day soon went and I got home and slammed the door. I threw my bag on the floor, sat on the couch snoring.
Who would be me?

***Cheryle Hall (9)***
***Field End Junior School***

## A DAY IN THE LIFE OF A BOY

I got up at five
felt like a drive,
Just went six
just had my Weetabix.

Now it was seven
I nearly floated up to Heaven.
Just got to school
lucky me - broke another rule.

Went to the Headteacher
what a horrible creature.
Wanted to go home
but I had to go to the Millennium Dome.

Went to my sister
'Oh no! Not another blister!'
Went for a swim
met a girl in my class called Kim.

Just got home
Guess what? It was the phone!
Got up the stairs, my sister was incredible
while my mum went to the doctors for a medical.
Looked at my dad - what a couch potato!
So I went upstairs and played with my Inflato.

We just had a stunning piece of beef
went upstairs to do my teeth.
Went downstairs to sit on my mum
I was eating chocolate cake, 'Yum, yum!'
I'm afraid it's time . . .
I wonder, would you like a life like mine?

***Rhys Williams (9)***
***Field End Junior School***

## A Day In The Life Of Frank Lampard

7.00am I wake up, I have a shower. Shove my shirt on, smack on those shorts, roll up the long socks, get the boots on. Get the training jacket. Wait just outside the front gates until the coach picks me up and takes me to the ground at 8.30am. Then get ready, don't be nervous. I have friends called Steve Lomas, Neil Ruddock, Paulo Wanchope, Paulo Di Canio, Impey, Bywater, Shaka Hislop and Craig Forrest. The last three are the goal-keepers.

My dad is called Frank . . . Senior. Find the middle, take the senior away and you will find me. I play for West Ham and I have about 60 caps. I've scored about 30 goals. I'm 21 years old and my number is 18.

My car is a snazzy Jaguar. I have smooth black hair, as black as pitch midnight. I'm quite rich in fact I'm very rich. I'm very famous. My football trainer is Harry Rednap - do you know who I am? Yes! You've guessed it, I'm Frank Lampard. The best midfielder out of the whole of the West Ham squad. If you're thinking of playing for West Ham and you're under 16 join up at the U9s, U10s and U11s and more join up now.

West Ham are the best!

***Christopher Bolwell (9)***
***Field End Junior School***

## A DAY IN THE LIFE OF A CAT

Dear Aunt Kitty

I slept out last night in the alleyway; during the night I woke up to find a dog looking me in the eye. Once I'd escaped into the garden I was parched, but there was no water, so I had to do with a mouse. Then finally I was let in. You know I'm still going to Doctor Fluffy to try to stop me going for the annoying bird I live with. He looks so tasty though. Instead of him, I am having lamb in jelly, it's my absolute favourite, it comes in this can with Whiskers written on it.

After that I snuck in one of the bedrooms for some peace away from all the commotion. Do you know what I mean? Anyway, I fell asleep on the bed. I was having a wonderful time. My sister Mog and I . . . we were princesses, we were the prettiest, fairest and kindest of them all. However, in my *romantic scene* . . . I was swung in the air. The reason was I was spotted in the bedroom and forced downstairs.

Oh one last thing, I've gotta tell you something hilarious that happened, the children's nan had come to babysit. The thing is she screams at the sight of mice. She was fine until Mog brought in a mouse and let it run round the house, you should have been there.

*Love Reebok*

***Ceri Gordon (9)***
***Field End Junior School***

## A Day In The Life Of Me . . .

Brrrr! The noisy alarm clock went off at 7.30am as usual, then I heard my mum yelling 'Get up! It's time to brush your teeth.'
However, we're still tired, moaning and groaning just a little longer.
'Why do we have to get up this early?'
Mind you, I'm the one who's always shouting 'Hurry up! We're going to be late.'
So as always, I get up. The time I go to bed on schooldays is 9.00pm.

We arrived at school today and it was the day that we were going to find out who our teacher was going to be in year five.

Before that we had to write about a day in the life of . . . I chose to do Nicole Panayi. It was Friday afternoon. By the end of the day I was told that my teacher was going to be Mr Stringer.

The school day was over and I had to go home. We ate our dinner at 5.00pm, and we go to bed at whatever time we are told to.

***Nicole Panayi (9)***
***Field End Junior School***

## A DAY IN THE LIFE OF MYSELF

I woke up at six
to find I was in a fix.
I brushed my teeth
after I ate my beef.
I went to school
but I broke the rule.
So I got told off
so I sprinted off.
I went to the shops
in a bit of a hop.
I went in the cleaning room
to find a rusty broom,
I went back to class
to find windows made of glass.
Now it was ten
I dropped my pen
With a bit of a spray
it was time to play.
At three it was time to go
I bought a ball to throw
Already it was five
the bees were buzzing in their hive.
Now it was nine -
Would you like a life like mine?

***Wilson Tang (9)***
***Field End Junior School***

## A Day In The Life Of Stephanie

7.00am

My dad dragged me out of bed and when he went, I jumped back in and pulled the covers over me. He called me, he shouted 'Get up now, you will be late!' About three minutes later he shouted again 'Are you up yet?' So up I got 'I don't want to go to school,' I replied.
'Why not?'
'Because we have a new teacher called Ms Funnybone and new people called Chatalot!'

So off I went with some friends.
'Look, look, there's Mrs Friedface with Ms Funnybone. Look she is going to blow the whistle!' So in we went.

Soon it was lunch time, after lunch we had Art, we made Roman soldiers after which Mrs Funnybone read us a story, then it was the end of the day.

***Stephanie Worthy (9)***
***Field End Junior School***

## A Day In The Life Of A Newt

'Hi, I'm Ned the newt, at the moment I'm being chased by a bird.'
'Whaaa!' He almost had my foot there, better dive under the water.
Phew! He's gone away now. It's summer at the moment.
Ahggh! You know what that means . . . ? Children! I hate them, they're always picking me up or accidentally catching me in their fishing nets.

Better hide - here they come, I'll have to do my trick . . . Step forward, step back, quick swerve and away to the end of the river. Oh look a water hopper - I'll eat him. I'm right under him. Snap, snap! I've got him . . . that was nice. I think I'll go and sit on a Lilypad. Oh no I won't, anything could get me. But oh great! No one around, cool shady water. Yes! I think I'll have a nice little nap. What may I ask is wrong with a newt's life?

***Harry Saunders (9)***
***Field End Junior School***

## A Day In The Life Of Martin Luther King

Martin Luther King set up a Civil Rights Organisation for the black people. In that time in America, black people weren't as well paid as the white people. He thought this was unfair - this is his speech (an extract).

*'I have a dream that one day this Nation will rise up and live out the true creed. We hold these truths to be self evident; that all men are created equal!'*

'Today's a big day,' he said as he walked towards the kitchen for breakfast. He sat down slowly and opened the newspaper.
*'Martin's big speech!'* it said on the front cover.
'I'm on the front of every damn newspaper!' he said.
'Are you ready sir?' said the bodyguard.
'Hold on!'

He and the bodyguard walked to the door and into the car, not knowing what would happen!

(A longer extract)

*'I have a dream that one day on the red hills of Georgia the sons of former slaves, and the sons of former slave owners, will be able to sit down at the table of Brotherhood*

*I have a dream that one day my four children will live in a Nation where they will not be judged on the colour of their skin, but the content of their character!'*

Bang!

The whole crowd were shocked to find that Martin Luther King has been assassinated at the very young age of 39.

***Nirmal Trivedy (10)***
***Field End Junior School***

## A Day In The Life Of James Bond's Stunt-Double

'Gulp!' said Pierce Brosnan as he looked over the big drop.
'What're you gulping for?' asked his stunt-double Jim, looking himself, 'you've only got to have a punch-up with Dr Evil!'
'Yes, but he wins, throws me over the edge and then . . .' his voice faded away.
'Don't worry about that, you don't have to do that, I have to. I'm your stunt-double, remember!' he exclaimed.
'Oh yeah, do you get to do the punch-up?' he asked.
'More like claw-up!' Dr Evil laughed.
'That's not funny' said Q handing stunt-double Jim a grapple hook to catch the top of the building as he falls to the ground.

'Alright people, let's get moving!' the director shouted.
'Lights, camera and action . . . !'
They started the punch-up. Dr Evil put a great punch to the jaw of Pierce.
'Stunt-double fill in!'
Stunt-double ran in and slid down the roof and fell off.
He got out his grapple hook, threw it up. It missed.
He landed on the trampoline.
Just as he got to the lift door, it opened and there was a man saying
'You're fired!'

A day later Jim Graham was standing on the roof and he found the old grapple hook. He jumped. There was no trampoline there anymore. He threw the old rusty grapple hook, it caught the edge. Crack! There was a crack in the grapple hook and it broke. But he didn't fall, he looked up and saw a man holding the end!

The man pulled him up and set him safely on the roof.
'Who are you? And thank you!' Jim said.
'I'm Rob the new stunt-double!' the man answered.

***Jon Platt (10)***
***Field End Junior School***

## A Day In The Life Of Pat The Pencil

My day begins in the drawer with all my friends, Percy the pen, Edward the eraser, Ron the ruler and my true love, Sabrina the scissors.

First Bill would put me in his bag, ready for school. In there I would have to wear a gas-mask because it really smells of banana skins and rotten sandwiches.

Once my friends and I are at school Bill takes Percy the pen, Edward the eraser, Ron the ruler and me out and starts using us. This is our daily routine apart from weekends.

Anyway, we were in school and this is how my day began.

'Ouch! Ouch! This paper is really thick. Ow! Ow!' shouted Sabrina
'What is it?' I replied.
'Bill's using me to cut this piece of very thick card and he's hurting me!'
'Oh, don't worry, he's stopped now!' said Sabrina.
Then there was a horrible smoky smell and a deafening alarm bell was heard. I grabbed Sabrina and all of us got out.
The school had caught on fire, all the adults and children were screaming even Bill was.

When we got home, Bill got all the attention of course. Well nobody even knows we're alive, so how could we be looked after?

A day had passed from the moment when the school had caught on fire and my friends and I were on the window ledge. Then suddenly a huge gust of wind threw me out of the window and into the drain. It was so smelly in there, even smellier than in Bill's school bag which was pretty bad anyway.

Finally after floating in those mucky pipes, there was a light. Quickly I climbed out of the drain and came out onto the road.

Then as fast as you could say *stop!* A car just drove straight over me and cracked me in half. I was left there for 15 hours until Bill came walking down the road. He saw me and picked me up. When I was home, Bill mended me with sellotape and put me with all my friends again, safely on his shelf.

***Natasha Caine (10)***
***Field End Junior School***

## A Day In The Life Of James Starling

It was in the year of 1941, the Second World War had been on for two years and the HMS Starling (the submarine I was on) had made it through a hit 'n' run mission. This is where my story begins . . .

We were doing a little dodging from the depth charges the boat above was dropping.
'Cut the engine, cut the engine!' It all went quiet. The boat moved off right into our sights.
'Fire torpedoes one and two,' I whispered.
Thomas Cardon flicked two switches, and two fast torpedoes shot off and blew up the back of the boat. We had a direct hit. Three minutes later we got word that the boat was 'Ull Shlachenfeíl', it had sunk nine submarines in two days.
We began to celebrate at our accomplishment. No one saw the sinking ship ahead. As we hit it the front of our sub began to buckle.

Thomas came into our meeting room with blood on his face and a limp arm at his side.
'The front of the sub's severely damaged and there is too much pressure in the torpedo chutes, they're going to explode!'
I thought about this.
'H . . . how's Douglas?' I stuttered.
'Alright.'
'Well, I want everyone to be fitted with life jackets. We're going to surface.'
Thomas limped away hollering, 'Code red, life jackets on!'
A few minutes later there was a jolt as we surfaced. I went up the turret, opened the hatch and 'Schnéll Von Stañcón!' The Germans had us surrounded, there was no escape. The soldiers came and shoved us all on the boat. As the Germans began to get into our sub, a smile grew across my face. The boat's engines started and we moved off. When we were a mile away, there was a huge explosion where our sub had been. Suddenly, I saw the butt of a gun and then everything went black.

I awoke, lying on a cold, stone floor, in a prison cell. I wasn't alone, there was Thomas Cardon, Jeffery Lagger and Douglas Bader, with his hard wooden legs. He seemed to be hacking at something.

‘Where are we, and what are you doing?’ I asked Douglas.
‘Colditz, and I’ve found a tunnel, we’ll be able to escape tonight.’

At approximately 11.00pm we gathered our stuff and went into the hole. We came out just beyond the wall. When everything was clear, we ran. We ran as fast as we could until we came to the edge of a wood. We could hear the sirens screeching and the loading of the guns. We slowly crawled deep into the wood.

A few days later we came to France. After talking to the locals, we found out where the French resistance was. We had to go into the an swé shop and down into the cellar, where we would meet the general.

‘Hi-we-wish-to-go-back-to-England.’ I said. The general looked at me as if I was stupid.
‘I talk English and we’ve got a boat waiting.’
‘Oh thanks!’ I saluted him and then we left for the boat. After a long, rocky trip (and a couple of attacks from the Germans, in which we lost Jeffery, a very good friend) we finally got back to England and we were all reassigned to a new sub which would take us on yet another adventure.

***Damian Holland (10)***
***Field End Junior School***

## A Day In The Life Of Dylan The Dog

One summer's morning Katie, Lauren, Sophie, Mick, Nikki and Dylan thought they would go for a walk through the field. Katie's dad let the dog off on a very long string lead. When they were going through the long grass, Katie's dad let go of the lead without thinking so when they got home they finally realised that they had left Dylan the dog behind. So they ran all the way back to the field and he wasn't there, anywhere, so they searched and they searched till it got dark.

What Dylan had done was, he had found a new owner. So the lady phoned 0207 111 1111 and Katie answered the phone. It was the lady saying 'I have got your abandoned dog.' They were so pleased that they went to her house immediately. Once they had got Dylan back, they were so relieved, but the dog didn't want to come home. They had trouble, but in the end they gave up. But they had a happy life with him until he died. He was having trouble with his eyesight, so the vet gave him some antibiotics to help him see. When they went back to the vets he said he had cancer and two weeks later Dylan died. They were so upset because he was only 2½ years old. In the end they got another dog, but he also died so they didn't bother getting any more dogs.

They did get a kitten and a rabbit. But Katie really liked dogs so her mum and dad said to her that for her birthday present in August, they would get her another dog. They were so excited about getting a dog, a few weeks passed by and they got a dog.

***Lauren Arnold (10)***
***Field End Junior School***

## A Day In The Life Of Dennis Wise

The England squad is training in Belgium and Dennis Wise doesn't know if he is playing on Tuesday against Romania. England have to win or draw to get through to the quarter-finals. Romania look good and so do England, I think this match is going to be a very tight match. If England play the way they played against Germany, I think they will win but if they play like they played against Portugal, Romania have got a very good chance.

Dennis Wise is a brilliant player and Kevin Keegan likes him so I think he will start for England. He may not last for the whole game so I think that he will put Nick Barmby on for Wise. Dennis Wise was training the other day and he looks in good shape, although this morning he had stomach pains. Shearer looks very good for this match and it looks like England have got a good chance. Kevin Keegan thinks that England are in brilliant shape, especially Michael Owen. Owen is as fit as ever. My prediction for this match - I think the score will be 2-1 to England. I think that Dennis Wise will get the first goal and Owen will get the second. Romania's best player is out with an injury. That player is Hagi but he will be fit to play the next game in the quarter-finals if they get through. England have got one more training session when Kevin Keegan picks Dennis Wise or Nick Barmby. I love seeing Dennis Wise play, so I hope he will choose Wise. I think Dennis Wise is my football hero. Nick Barmby is a good football player but I want Wise to start the game. I don't know why Kevin Keegan hasn't even picked Andy Cole instead of Emile Hesky because Andy Cole has scored about 20 goals for Manchester United and Emile Hesky has scored four goals for Leicester and Liverpool.

***Josh O'Neill (10)***
***Field End Junior School***

## A DAY IN THE LIFE OF TILLY

Hi, my name is Tilly and I am fluffy, soft and I have silky fur. I am light grey, with dark grey stripes.

I can be very friendly, especially to my owners, Courtenay, Chelsea, Ryan, John and Mandy. They all look after me very well. I bet you have guessed already that I am a cat.

I have a brother called Chip (he is a twin), we also live with this dog called Roxy.

It's really fun being a cat because you can do anything you want. You can go out, stay in, play with your owners or ever lie on their laps, now that is the life! It is cosy and nice, you should try it sometime. I mean if you were a cat, like me.

My brother always goes out but I prefer to stay in or lie outside in the sun. Sometimes Courtenay's friends come round. Let me think, there is Carly, Rebecca, Chloe, Katie, Nicola and Alex. Sometimes other people come round they are Chelsea's friends. There's Ashleigh, Elizabeth, Katherine and loads more. There are even more of Ryan's friends, Paris, Peter, Andrew and even Natalie! I always see Ryan, John and Mandy but I only see Chelsea and Courtenay on weekends.

First the kids go to bed and Mandy and John are still up (so are we) and then they go to bed (so do we). Me, Chip and Roxy sleep on the beds, I sleep on Chelsea's bed, Chip sleeps on Courtenay's bed and Roxy sometimes sleeps on Ryan's bed or she sleeps on John and Mandy's bed. We are all happy where we sleep.

In the morning someone comes down to feed us, *yummy!* Me and Chip get lovely food but I don't know about Roxy! Roxy can be rude sometimes, she might, while they are eating, chase them if they have food in their hands (I think that is funny). Chip does not see it because he is always out. That is the end of a day in the life of me, Tilly, bye!

***Courtenay Hilmi (19)***
***Field End Junior School***

## A DAY IN THE LIFE OF TJ

One morning at 4.00am TJ got up and went outside and he saw Stumpy the bully.
Stumpy said 'Get out of town and don't come back!'
Then TJ got so scared he did get out of town. Rebecca and Aaron the owners of TJ called him but TJ did not come. They kept on calling him every morning but he still didn't come. So Rebecca decided to make a missing sign, saying:-

Missing - cat, black and white with a bright yellow collar.
If you find him please call 0208 868 4105.

TJ was walking around and saw some other cats and all they did was hiss at him. He saw a mouse but TJ was not in the mood to eat him. TJ went in an alley and stayed there for four days without any food or water. Rebecca called TJ but there was no sign of him. Stumpy's gang went nowhere near Stumpy.

So Stumpy said 'I've got to go and find TJ,' and he did eventually find him and said 'Do you want to be my partner?'
TJ looked shocked, he said 'Me and you partners?'
Yes that is right! Stumpy and TJ - partners.
'But there's one thing you have to do, stay away from your parents.'
'No I can't, they love me so much. I can't, Rebecca and Aaron would be awfully upset.'
'Do you want to be cool or not?'
'No!' said TJ
He rushed home as fast as he could. Miaow, TJ is back. Don't lie, TJ and Rebecca and Aaron lived happily ever after. But I can tell you something. TJ isn't the one getting bullied!

***Katie Lecky (10)***
***Field End Junior School***

## A Day In The Life Of Bart Simpson

I had a dream last night as a day in the life of Bart Simpson - here it is.

'Wake up Bart!' his mum said, 'you will be late for school.'
'Phew, made it just in time!' said Bart
'Hey Millhouse do you want ten pounds?'
'Yeh!'
'OK!'
'Ooo ee, ahh, ahh, OK Bart, I can only handle three.'
'Oh yeh I knew that, how come I forgot?'
'OK kids!'
'OK class I hope you have revised for your SATs test.' explained the teacher.
'Oh no, I forgot!'
'Oh well, Bart what a surprise!'
'Oh well you will have to have an 'F grade', won't you Bart? And that is a week's detention for not revising for SATs.'
'Oh man, I won't be able to see radioactive man, series 14 now!' said Bart.
'I'll bring it into school for you.' said Millhouse.
'Ah, thanks Millhouse!'
'That's OK Bart.'
'Hmm this test is really hard.'
'OK class!' says the teacher, '10 minutes.'
'Oh no, I'll quickly change with the smart kids.' Thinks Bart.
'Oh Bart you have finished what a surprise!'
'I'm just going to the principal's office, Bart's cheated. This writing's too neat and clear.' said the teacher.
'We'll suspend him for a year, he will be shocked.'
'Bart you're suspended for one year.'
'Uh,' the class said.
Bart told his mum and dad but they did not listen and that was it and I'm glad I'm not Bart Simpson.

***James King I10)***
***Field End Junior School***

## A Day In The Life Of A British Airways Air Stewardess

At 5.30am the alarm goes off. She gets up and gets herself ready for the long day ahead. She's off to Phoenix today. She gets in her car and drives to Gatwick. She checks in and goes to meet the cabin crew on her flight. She gets on the bus that takes her to the aeroplane. She checks the plane and then the passengers board the plane.

5, 4, 3, 2, 1 ready for take-off. Once they are up in the air she puts the films on. While the films are showing, the meals are being heated. She goes and serves the drinks, when she comes back, the meals are ready for serving.
'Chicken or beef?' is the famous call. A few minutes later she's round again.
'Tea or coffee, sir?' She's always on the move even 30,000 feet in the air.
It's time to clear away the trays, so out she goes again with her trolley.
Once all the trays are cleared away, the lights go down and the passengers can watch the movies in peace. This is now the time that she can have a rest if she's lucky! There are beds at the back of the plane for the crew to sleep in. But only for one or two hours. She then gets back to work and now it's time for the afternoon teas. Another trolley comes out to be pushed up the aisle and more tea or coffee. She has to work quickly because there isn't much time until the plane is due to land. She has lots of paperwork to complete before the plane lands in Phoenix. Rush, rush rush, she then goes around with green waiver forms for the passengers to fill in. It's not long now, everyone is strapped in, the call for the cabin crew to sit in their special seat goes out. Suddenly they've landed in sunny Phoenix.

After making sure all the passengers are safely off the plane she can finally get off the plane. She waits for her bags with the rest of the crew and they all get on the bus that takes them to the hotel for a well-earned sleep.

Phoenix is 8 hours behind London, so she tries to keep awake a little longer so she does not wake up in the middle of the night.

***Hayley Weaver (9)***
***Field End Junior School***

## A Day In The Life Of Me

8.00am:
The doorbell went. My alarm went off and I smashed it with my hammer that I keep under my pillow. My mum called me about 12 times.
'Get downstairs now!'
I dashed downstairs, gobbled up my breakfast. Afterwards I zoomed to school, I was just in time!

It is Tuesday and we are doing art. We made a person, painted it and put hair on it. Then I went home, played football with Jack. Then I went on my bike. After tea I went to tennis and had a good time. While I was there I learnt how to serve. When my lesson finished I got into the car and my mum drove me home. At home I had a big bubbly bath after which I got into my bed and listened to my tape. Then I fell asleep.

***Oliver Michaelson (9)***
***Field End Junior School***

## A Day In The Life Of Alan Shearer

Today was the big day, England V Germany in Euro 2000. The time everyone had been waiting for, had arrived! The team were nervous but very confident, including me, Alan. In the morning Michael had announced. 'Everyone is counting on me and I won't let them down.' England haven't beat Germany for 33 years and this was our big chance. We needed to win this match if we wanted to get into the quarter-final.

Now the time was drawing near and we were all in our kits. Today we were playing in red because England and Germany usually play in white.

Me, Michael, David and the rest of the England team, had a team discussion before we went on. I was too busy thinking about the game to sing the National Anthem, but the crowd gave me a lot of support. The flags went off and everybody was cheering and shouting.

Both England and Germany got into their positions and our ninety minutes started. In the first half nothing really happened, in fact it was quite boring, we only had a few chances of scoring. I really thought it was going to turn out as a draw, but luckily it didn't!

In the second half it turned out the complete opposite. We had a good chance of scoring and I took our big chance. David Beckham passed me the ball and with a great header, I changed the score to 1-0 to England, I felt brilliant! The crowd had gone mad and we were just praying Germany wouldn't score.

Now we were in injury time and the final whistle went. We were thrilled! It had been so long since we had beaten them and after 33 years, 10 months, 18 days, 4 hours, 17 minutes at last we had beaten them!

***Nicola Bates (10)***
***Field End Junior School***

## A Day In The Life Of Julie The Maid

'Julie come in please.'
'Yes, my lady!'
'You will be working in the kitchen with the other maids from now on only because your friend has been given the sack.'
Julie was happy because the kitchen was decorated with herbs on the wall. It also had a lovely smell to it. Then another maid got called into the big living room.
'You will not be working in the kitchen, you will be working around the house.'
Then the doorbell rang.
'Ah that must be my sister!'
'Julie, come here.'
'Yes!'
'Would you show my sister around the house so she feels at home?'
'OK!'
'First I will show you your room, then I will show you to your own bathroom and then to the living room.'
'Thank you dear!'
'Now I need to get back to work in the kitchen.'

*A month later!*

'Ouch!'
'What on earth is going on?'
'I've just burnt myself.'
'How?'
'On a saucepan.'
'Well you didn't have to scream that loud!'
'I know but it really hurt.'
Everyone came out and left the pots on the fire, they didn't know that Julie's pot caught fire. All of a sudden the fire alarm went off and all the maids had to get everyone out who was important and then the maids ran out screaming. The firemen came to put out the fire and said.
'It was a big saucepan that caught alight'
The queen was furious with Julie because she knew it was Julie's pot that caught alight.

'Why did you leave the saucepan on the gas?'
'Because I thought the other maids could turn it off for me.'
'You were wrong, so you are fired!'
'Fine I'll just go to another castle who appreciate me.'
A week later Julie got a job at another castle. She was then asked to go back to her old job of working for the queen but Julie said 'No I am working here until I retire.'

***Alex Pearce (10)***
***Field End Junior School***

## THE DAY IN THE LIFE OF SHEEN, THE HORSE

Sheen the horse passed today and there was another horse but I don't know the other horse's name. It is because Sheen is my special horse from my farm. I let people borrow him on a special occasion like on a wedding but not bad people because they might hurt those poor horses especially Sheen, if he goes I will get upset. He is a precious horse to me and my family. If he has gone, we will be crying for days. But we want to go and feed him.

Amy Pollock is my best friend, she feeds him whenever she wants. My other best friend is called Danny. My friend Ryan is so nice to me and I say you can feed him. Well one day he was gone. We phoned up the police and they said they would try to find Sheen. I was crying for days, Amy said it will be alright. Danny was crying because he won't be able to feed him until they find him. The police said that he might be stolen by a man. We had to have him back for tomorrow for a wedding. If he does not come back that means nobody will like using Sheen anymore so we said to the police, can you try and find Sheen by tomorrow. 'Yes we will try to get him.'

He came back thank God, so he went to the ceremony and he was the best horse in town. Everybody loved Sheen and we got lots of money and we were famous and we were happy.

***Laura Loxton (9)***
***Field End Junior School***

## A Day In The Life Of Alan Shearer

Alan Shearer came on for the England side. Shearer and Owen took kick-off. Germany tried to get the ball but England passed and passed to each other. Germany got the ball. They had a shot but Seaman saved it. He booted it down field to Beckham who kicked it down to Owen. Thirty minutes gone, Owen to Scholes. Scholes had a shot, just hit the post and the ball went to Shearer.

In the changing rooms at half-time, Shearer was getting mad and Kevin Keegan was getting mad at Shearer. In the second half Shearer was getting the ball lots of times. Owen got fouled - free kick to England. Shearer was in there, Beckham crossed it. Dennis Wise headed it to Shearer. Shearer headed it in - 1-0 to England. The crowd were saying Shearer, Shearer.

The second half went quickly. We had two substitutes, Owen, Shearer and Wise had a chance but missed. After ninety minutes the whistle was blown. The match for Shearer and his team mates ended 1-0 to them.

The team had a laugh at the end of the match. The team were so happy that they won 1-0 against Germany so they went on to Romania but they lost 3-2.

***Ben Hunter (10)***
***Field End Junior School***

## A DAY IN THE LIFE OF A TEACHER

I woke up at 6:00 in the morning.
How boring.
I got dressed and brushed my teeth,
I looked outside to see a thief.
I got in the car to go to school
Never to know that I bumped into the wall.
Before school I met a very naughty boy,
In school the children filled me with joy.
I told off two little girls
For their hair was full of golden curls.
At break in the staff room
I found a silver magic broom.
In my class Jack ate his pen,
Then he brought me a golden hen.
The next lesson is lunch
The children punch.
Lucy got punched
Then I found Pokémon cards, a whole bunch.
In the staffroom it's extremely cold,
It reminded me I was getting old.
I had my lunch, mmm ham roll and a chocolate bar.
A child in my class ran away really far;
I nearly got the sack for that,
After school I brought a hat.
My husband brought a scout's knife,
Would you like my life?

***Peaches Demetriou (9)***
***Field End Junior School***

## A Day In The Life Of My Cat, Chester

Today Chester my cat woke up at 7:01. He decided to go downstairs to have some breakfast with my other cat Charlie who had just woken up as well. Then, I got up, when I went in the kitchen Chester started yapping. I let him out and he started playing on the grass with Charlie.

Then, he walked round to the front, by this time it was about 9:30. He played and fought out there for about one and a half hours. He decided to take a sleep under the tree in our front garden.

When he woke up he jumped onto the front window sill and waited for someone to open the window to let him in. When he came in he jumped on the chair by the window then jumped straight off again and ran into the kitchen to get some lunch with Charlie (12:30).

When he had finished his lunch, he and Charlie went upstairs and jumped on a bed. Then they went to sleep until about 3:30 then they came down to get some biscuits.

When they had finished they played outside until they got hungry again (about 6:30). After they had had their dinner they could go out the back for a bit. Then they came in for the night and went to sleep on a bed. They went back out again at about 4:30am.

***Sam Pearce (10)***
***Field End Junior School***

## A DAY IN THE LIFE OF MY HAMSTER, CHIP

Deno woke up and saw Chip. Bob tried to hurt him, but Chip jumped back into his cage. Nelson had just woken up from his sleep and told Bob off.

Chip got out of his cage and jumped up to see Nelson and said 'Thank you Nelson for telling Bob off.'

Chip wanted to play in the garden. Deno told Chip to watch out for Bob. Chip replied 'OK.'

Deno was splashing about when he saw Bob run extremely fast out into the green grass garden. Deno shouted at Nelson, 'Quick, quick.' Bob ran extremely fast out into the garden, *'Help Chip and do it quick!'*

Nelson whispered to Deno. 'You jump up and down saying come and eat me I am tastier than Chip then Bob will come and get you. I'll pull this bit of string and the fly swat will fall down then Chip can get in his cage.'

So that was the terrifying job. Chip got back in his cage. Bob had to move the hamster cage next to the fish tank.

Deno was playing with Nelson when Bob opened the cage and got his claw and scraped Chip who was bleeding bad.

When Chip got healed by Deno and Nelson, Bob heard the humans and yelled, 'Back to your places our owners are back.'

Everyone went back to their places and when their owners got back, Bob was snuggled up and so was Chip, plus Deno and Nelson . . .

***Ryan Endacott (9)***
***Field End Junior School***

## A DAY IN THE LIFE OF A LEOPARD

I woke up to a loud *bang* from a gun this morning. There are more hunters in the wild than there are leopards. My family have already been killed by those hunters, I'm the only leopard in the family that's left. They are going to catch me in their trap of slaughtering death. They are now running towards me! I have to get up, I have to run, I have to hide, but where shall I run? Where shall I hide? Around here is only trees and bushes. But I have no time to think, I have to escape, quick, I have to escape now! I'll jump in this bush and I will be safe. I made it!
'Where did he go?' shouts one of the hunters.
'Don't just stand there, look for him! Wait a minute, what's that tail coming out of the bush? Why it's the . . .'
'Shut up, you will frighten him and he'll escape!'
They will never find me in here.
'You stand there and make sure he doesn't escape and I'll creep up and shoot him with the sleeping dart and then hey presto! He'll be our main attraction in London Zoo.'
'He'll do very well.'
'OK are you behind me?'
'Yes'
'Let's start'
Oh no! They have found . . .
'Got him, he's sleeping like a baby . . .'
Where am I? It's a zoo. They weren't trying to kill me! Wait, there's my family. They're not dead either!

***Jessica Brownlee (10)***
***Field End Junior School***

## A DAY IN THE LIFE OF 007

Bee-beep, bee-beep 'Oh shut up! Shut up you stupid alarm clock! OK then I'll switch you off! Oh! This is such an unpleasant dream! Oh well . . . I guess it's time to get up! Oh I must have overslept and I'd better be getting off!'

Five minutes later in 007's car . . .

'Ah! Dum dee doo dum da doo da day! Hey that big building over there! It must be our new meeting place. 006 said that he was trying to get a nicer meeting place!'

Later in the meeting place . . .

'Hello 006, I'm sorry I was late . . . I guess I must have overslept.'
'When will you learn not to sleep over your alarm clock 007? You're late nearly every day! Anyway, no time for arguing 007, we have got a mission to accomplish!'
'Oh but . . .'
'No time for buts 007, General Oromouv is planning to fire the Goldeneye, the Goldeneye will regenerate the Earth back to the stone age and you must do something fast! You hear that? I said fast and not sleeping over your alarm clock!'
'OK I'm moving!'
'OK 007, then here's the mission plan. OK then Oromouv, you're done for!'

Meanwhile at the dam . . .

'A pleasant day isn't it your Russian Infantry'
'Yes! Lovely isn't it. Hey what did I hear?'
'The name's Bond, James Bond!'
*Bang, bang, bang! Meowm!*
'There . . . better get moving to that platform over there for the big bungee jump! Aaarrrggghhh!'

Twenty seconds later . . .

'Aaarrrggghhh! That sure did hurt! Well at least I landed in the air vent so I can meet 006 in the science lab. Now all I have to do is get to that door over there without letting anyone see me. Here goes . . . ah! Done now I have to meet 006 in the bottling room.'

Five minutes later.

'Ah! Hello 006, it's time to blow up the tanks of gas. OK 006, you wait by the door. Let's see . . .'
5, 4, 3, 2, 1, 0, *kaboom!*
'Quick 006 . . . run! Oh no . . . 006 didn't make it.'

Three days later in the cradle . . .

'Right! The final battle between me and Oromouv! This is going to be good!'
'Greetings James!'
'Huh! That's not Oromouv, that's 006! That's right 006, back from the dead!'
'You killed me so I'll kill you!'
'OK then 006, but I shall not lose.'
*Meowm! Bang! Kaboom!*
'Hey 006, I thought it was a joke! Well then I guess it's pay-back time!'
*Kaboom! Meowm! Meowm! Bang! Bang!*
'Hey! It's not a dream after all! Well I couldn't care less, I'm going to bed.'

***James Bowers (10)***
***Field End Junior School***

## A Day In The Life Of A Cat

I woke up this morning and felt something long and furry by my back. It was a tail. When I got out of bed I was walking on all fours, I was all furry and I had whiskers. I'm a cat, I couldn't believe it, just think about it, I don't have to go to school or anything.

I think I will go and sit by the fire, ahhh this is really nice. I'm so warm and comfy it's so much better than going to school. I wonder, shall I go and wreck Mr Snells' rose garden?

When I was little he popped my favourite ball on purpose because I kicked it over into his garden by accident. My mum was furious and we have been rivals ever since.

Hmm I enjoyed that a lot. When I'm human I wonder if he will pay me to straighten out his flowers. Well I might as well go home and have some kitty fish and a drink.

That night when I went to bed my tail got caught and in the morning it was on the floor and I had a stump where my tail had been pulled off so I have never worn tight trousers again.

***Helen Gillen (10)***
***Field End Junior School***

## MR AND MRS OWL

Mr Owl woke up early in the morning and was talking to Mrs Owl. Mr Owl had some beans on toast with Mrs Owl and said, 'Oh how lovely the day is today. I'm going to take a walk to see Mr Badger, be back soon.'
'Please can I come, maybe we can have a picnic. I've got bread for sandwiches.'
'Maybe, I think I'm just going to take a shower, I'm ready.'
'Let's go then.'
'Careful getting down, have you got the tea?'
'Yes.'
'How about this. isn't this a nice spot?'
'May I have a sandwich?'
'We won't go to see Mr Badger we'll go another time. We still want dinner.'
'Yes, I'll go and get the mouse.'
'Let's go now.'

Halfway down to the mouse, *bang, bang, bang,*
'Help!'
'Yes I'm home at last, Oh no, what's happened to my husband, he's dead.'
'I'm not dead, I fainted. I'm OK now. I laid down because of the shooting. Make some toast please. I'll be alright, in fact I'm going straight to bed, goodnight.'
I hope he's alright.

***Stuart Sims (10)***
***Field End Junior School***

## A Day In The Life Of David Beckham

I would wake up and before I go to his house I would wash and have a bath, then have breakfast and get there for ten o'clock. After that I would drive in his car for about three or four hours and then I would go and train with Manchester United for two or three hours and then go to a restaurant. I would say to the waiter, 'Could I have prawn cocktail for starters, Yorkshire pudding, lamb for dinner and cake for desert?'

Then I would go shopping with Brooklyn Beckham and Victoria to buy some food and clothes and then go for a walk, then go to a friend's house. When I come back from my friend's house I would watch television. I would then fly to the country I was playing. I would then play for England or Manchester United. If I played for England I would fly to the country I was playing, I would play them and fly back. I would take a bath and go to bed.

***Jack Aylott (10)***
***Field End Junior School***

## A Day In The Life Of James Bond

As far as I can remember I had just come back from a mission in Istanbul. It was quite exciting to escape by air, again.

It felt excellent to be back in Britain. I was walking into MI6 headquarters. I noticed a man wearing shades, a black coat and he was holding a cigarette. He was staring at me. When I went in I greeted Moneypenny and M allowed me to come in.
'Good day M, did you miss me?' I asked.
'Yes 007, have you ever heard of molecular acid?'
I replied in my intelligent voice, 'Yes Sir, it is burning hot liquid capable of eating through any metal if I am right Sir.'
'Yes 007, two of our agents were found dead in Cairo last night, a cross burnt into their chest with the acid.'
I was very shocked by this.
'Your mission is to go to Cairo, find the problem and eliminate it. Please report to Q Branch.'

As I went to Q Branch I thought about the man outside MI6 and noticed how brief M was. He didn't even tell me when I was leaving for Cairo.
'Hello Q, any problems?' I asked him as I noticed his glasses.
'They're burning,' he said as he lazered through a wall with the glasses.
I will leave tomorrow morning early for Cairo where the mission begins.

***Matt Berryman (10)***
***Field End Junior School***

## A DAY IN THE LIFE OF PRISCILLA

The day began when my friend Nicola came round to go bike riding with me at 10:00am. She had ridden her bike to my house, which was a long way, so I let her in for a snack and a drink.

We were wondering where we should go bike riding when my sister, Chloe, shouted 'Wood, wood, wood.' She had given me a brainwave, we could go to the woods, which were nice and shady.

I went to the shed and got my mountain bike out. I propped it against the wall and went inside to pack my rucksack.

When that was done, we set off. I did not tell my mum where we were going. We were quite near the woods when it was 11:00am. I couldn't believe it, we had ridden our bikes for nearly an hour without eating anything. We stopped for a snack and a cool drink and carried on.

When we finally got to the woods, we tried to make a course but couldn't. There we met Alexandra who was also bike riding, but by herself. She helped design the course and make it. When it was finished, it looked perfect.

When 12:00pm finally came, we had a picnic. We shared our food between us. We were supposed to get back by 1:00pm but we stayed a bit later until 1:30pm. At 1:30pm I got a bit worried because the sky was dark and dull. I thought it was going to rain, so I suggested that we should go back to my house. We asked Alex if she could come with us. Alex answered, 'Yes, because my mum doesn't mind when I go back.'

It was when we were at the exit of the woods when the sun came out again. We decided to go home anyway as we were worried. When we were out of the woods, we found out that we were lost. All that we could see was a river with boats and bridge. We rode across the bridge, but as we did, it collapsed because we were too heavy for it. *Splash*, we fell in the river (well, I shouldn't be saying 'we' because Alex didn't even go on the bridge). Alex tried calling for help. In the end she gave up because nobody came.

By now, it was dark. In the end, Alex got the rope from our course and threw it into the river to let us tie it around our waists so she could haul us out.

When we were both out, we mopped ourselves with tissues. When we got home a few hours later, I had a quick shower and went downstairs. My big sister, Sarah asked, 'Where have you been?'
I answered glumly, 'To the woods.'
Chloe, my smallest sister said, 'Sissy, I missed you.'
Carmen, my small sister, older than Chloe, said nothing. It was very weird because she would normally say something after I'd been bike riding.

When Alex and Nicola had gone home, after having tea with us, Carmen said to me secretly, 'I'm sorry to say so, but I followed you.'
All I did was gasp.

***Priscilla Lok (10)***
***Field End Junior School***

## A Day In A Life Of A Rat

Tat the rat got up because of the racket up above
'Why am I the one who has to sleep under Stephen's house?'
Tat had a stretch and once again got held under the water by his brother James. 'Get off me. I'm going to the pet shop to see Bob, James.' When he got to the pet shop, someone had brought him.

The man glared at Tat and smiled. He had one good snatch and grabbed Tat. 'Leave me alone'
'A talking rat hey? Guess what I can sell you for? A basket of money!'
One day a boy named Paul came to the pet shop and brought Tat 'Help me, a talking rat.' The boy let Tat out and put him on his shoulder.

'Can you help me get home?'
'Yes I will.'
'Oi before I tell you where I live can you help me? Bob and I live in the sewers. Well can you help me find Bob and put him back in the pet shop?'

After Tat said that Paul said 'He's my dad!'
'Well then we better get going.' When Bob and Tat and Paul got there Bob stood in front of the man and said 'Give me my shop back'
'Well if you want it you'll have to pay me.' Bob paid the money and got his shop back and Paul took Tat back home to the sewers but suddenly Tat said to Paul 'Can I live with you?'
'Yes you can!' and after that they went back to Paul's house!

***Stephen Murton (9)***
***Field End Junior School***

## A Day In The Life Of A Butterfly

The cocoon snapped with noise. It fell to the bottom of the deep, deep floor. It fell in a heap of leaves and tried to fly.

There were ants coming through the dead leaves so the butterfly went for a fly and done it. It flew high high into the sky.

I, the butterfly ate some of someone's hat with leaves on. I landed on the grass and some people trapped me into a tub. They took me home and threw me right on to the floor with a big, big, big bang! I tried to make a hole in the bottom of the plastic tub. They lifted it up in the dark. They fell over . . . the table leg, with a great big crash! It was my chance to escape and fly into the corner. None of the doors or windows were open until . . . the friend opened the door to go out and I flew away. I flew as high as I could, until . . . I landed on top of a plane and the plane was just landing on the port. I had something to eat. I then had my last fly and fell to the floor and died.

***Emma Rigg (9)***
***Field End Junior School***

## A Day In The Life Of Tom Ted

There was once a girl named Charlotte, who just loved teddy bears. One July afternoon she found a teddy bear which had just been thrown on to the floor. Charlotte took the bear home and washed it. She said 'Mum, I found this bear and I've washed it up.' Charlotte went back to the park with her mum and Tom. Tom and Charlotte played in the sand pit. When they had to go Charlotte had such a lot of fun she had forgotten all about Tom. Tom had the same problem he had before!

Everybody was leaving him, what was he going to do? Was he ever going to find someone that will look after him? Then an old man came into the park, sat down on the bench and saw the bear. The old man was on his holidays. He went over to the bear, picked it up and thought my grandmother Rosie will love this. So the man went back to America a couple of days later and do you know what? Rosie loved him. They were as happy as can be. Tom thought that Rosie was a bit bossy but, on the other hand he still liked her. They baked cakes together, played in the sand, together. They always loved each other.

***Charlotte Baker (9)***
***Field End Junior School***

## A Day In The Life Of A Magical Fire

'Hi, Mum are we allowed to go to the pub in Leicester Square?'
Mum replied 'Yes, but you better look after your brother and sister.' So we set off down the road to the pub called The Small Swallow. We saw some monks set off a blazing fire, it looked like a magical fire. We then all rushed out of the pub to see the magical fire. Everybody went really really close and touched the magical fire and they all disappeared to somewhere that we didn't know anything about. Then Maisie, Jack and I went closer and closer and eventually we all touched it and we were thrown straight into an unknown land.

When we had got to this place we looked around, and we fell into a trap that zoomed all three of us up into a tree. We were stuck in this tree for over 6 or 7 hours, then we saw a load of Kindakoles that were laughing at us and lots of fierce and jumping tigers at our feet. Some of us escaped and saw this multicoloured circle, so we jumped through and we landed plum right in the middle of our beds fast asleep.

***Matthew Ayling (9)***
***Field End Junior School***

## THE TERMINATOR

It's 2098, in the future a man has made a terminator 'At last my greatest creation is completed *zzap*! The terminator is on!'
'I'm a terminator you are under my control;' shouted the terminator.
'Listen here terminator you're under my control . . . Ahh!'
'Ha ha ha ha' laughed the terminator and then stomped out of the lab.
'Comrade, I repeat Comrade, there is a man down there disguised as Arnold Schwarzenegger, there there!'
'Rrrr,' murmured the terminator.
'Watch out he's going to shoot.'
'Paul come down for tea,'
'Oh Mum;' and Paul stomped downstairs. 'Mmmm thanks Mum that was delicious;' and then Paul dashed upstairs.
'Aaaaa!' said Paul, 'I'm in the book and in the terminator body, I've got to go.'
I was trapped in a robot's body about to shoot at the RAF. I was the heart of the body I was wondering whether my mum was all right. But while I was thinking about my mum a gigantic missile was about to hit me, boom, I was in little pieces, the RAF people were cheering because they killed me. Then I came back together and went to Hawaii and partied until midnight. Suddenly I shot back to my mum and I was cuddling her.

***Paul Goodey (9)***
***Field End Junior School***

## A Day In The Life Of Chocolate Land

It was a hot Friday afternoon and Mum had come to pick us up from school. 'Hi guys,' Mum said in a cheerful voice.
'Hi Mum,' we said drearily.
'What's the matter?' Mum shouted.
'It's a lovely day and we were stuck in that old rusty building all day long,' Katie admitted.
'Oh well, the least I can do is get the pool out' Mum said.

'Mum, can we go the long way home and go the magical way?' Rhoswyn begged.
'Of course we can go the magical way,' Mum answered. We hit the road.

After half an hour a strange thing happened. Mum was real tired and she drove right into a bubble. 'Mum, where are we?' Rebecca asked in a funny sort of voice.
'I don't know but that house over there is made out of . . . chocolate, we must be in Chocolate Land' Mum screamed.
'Mum, there's a chocolate policeman heading straight towards us,' Katie cried. He came straight towards us and put our hands in handcuffs.
'Don't worry, we can bite through it' Mum smiled. So we did. It didn't take long. We started driving. 'Ow Mum, Rhoswyn hit me on the head' Rebecca said.
'No she didn't toffee apples are falling from the trees, I want to go home' Katie cried.
'OK let's find the bubble!' and we drove straight through it, and do you know what? we have still got a chocolate logo on the car.

***Jessica Williams (9)***
***Field End Junior School***

## )AY IN THE LIFE OF A POKÉMON TRAINER

It was a sunny day at Field End Junior School and Philip was playing on the grass. Suddenly he saw something small and bright near a bush, he went over and it was . . . a small piece of metal with a pattern on it. As soon as he touched it he was falling from the sky. He hit the ground with a thump! 'Where am I?' said Philip in total confusion. Meanwhile back at school . . .
'Mallory Hawkins, yep, John Dodon, yes, Josh Lev, Josh? Oh well Nicko Don, Nicko'
'Oh well.'
'Come on class let's get to work!'
Philip heard a voice it said 'Welcome to the world of Pokémon!'
In a booming voice 'Why am I wearing these funny clothes?' Philip said.
Before he said another word he was swept off the floor by some wild Pokémon and taken to a gym. He found balls on the floor and he threw them some. Pokémon came out and started attacking him and he was locked in! Then Josh and Nicko broke into the gym and frightened them away.

When they came out of the gym they were lost, then rocks started falling from the sky, and they ran to the nearest house and found a time machine. They closed their eyes and touched a button on the time machine, then next minute they were in the classroom.
'Boys! Where have you been?'

***Philip Upton (8)***
***Field End Junior School***

## A DAY IN THE LIFE OF A TEDDY BEAR

One night Jessica bought a new teddy, it was lovely and brown and had a beautiful blue in its eyes. She had called it Sammy. The night it had come when Jessica was asleep, Sammy was bullied by Fred, Ginger, Tiny and Blue Berry. Sammy was so upset that the next night the poor teddy ran away. In the morning Jessica was so upset that she didn't want to go to school but she had to. The next morning she was so upset that she wrote a notice saying :-

Lost Teddy
Please Find
Reward £100
Brown, Blue Eyes,
Small Ears

Sammy on the other hand was having as much luck as Jessica was, trying to find him. Sammy met a cat called Rachel, and she stayed at a garage, she purred to him 'You can stay with me for as long as you want.' Sammy was very grateful and stayed with her for two whole nights.

At night it was just right, it wasn't too cold and it wasn't too hot. Jessica and her really good friends were looking and when they went to the shops, guess what? she saw Sammy, and they both were really happy. From then on they went everywhere together except from school days because she would get told off badly! They went to the park together, they went to bed together, she never went to bed without him. She never ever went to a sleepover without him and they never lost each other ever again.

***Rebecca Simmons (9)***
***Field End Junior School***

## A Day In The Life Of Creepy The Ghost

In Ghost School the teacher was telling the ghosts where they were going to scare this year. 'Now these cards have got places where you are going to scare,' she explained.
'I got the cinema' said Creepy happily.
'That's good because it's near the park, we can meet at the cinema' said Slimy. Before Creepy met up with Slimy he saw what movies were on 'Ghost Terror' he read. That was the best movie. The second best movie was 'Monster Land.' Then Slimy came 'Sorry I'm late' he said tiredly.
'Where were you?' Creepy asked.
'I was at home and I forgot about you,' he explained.'
'Let's just go in' Creepy said. They were going in and monsters got in their way.
'Our friend is scaring here so go away!' they shouted.
'There's too much monster run' Slimy shouted. After they ran out of the cinema they tried to think how Creepy was supposed to do his scare.
'I know how about going to Wizards School to get a magic book?' Slimy asked.
'Good idea' replied Creepy. They rode off to Wizards School. When they got there they went straight to their secret underpass which they used a year ago. It led to the head teacher's office. Luckily the head teacher walked out. They grabbed 'the magic book of everything'. They used a spell to do their scares. They gave the book back but it had a curse. They had the best scares in school.

***Alex Rostocki (9)***
***Field End Junior School***

## A Day In The Life Of A Puppy

Chapter One - Wake Up

I, Alfie, woke up, hearing a dog. All of my brothers were climbing over me. I slowly got out of bed! 'I'm hungry' I went to the kitchen, jumped on the bar and nicked some food, munch munch.

'Mum, when can I go to the loo?' I was bursting to go so I went on the sofa. Then our owner came to let us out, his name is Luke. He let us out so I ran for it.

'Alfie!' I started to run because he was after me, soon he got me.

Chapter Two - Walkies

'Walkies!' Alfie went to his lead and slipped the collar on. Luke opened the door and we started to walk to the field. We were half way up there and Rex saw a Squirrel. Snap. Rex went running after the Squirrel. He then disappeared into the field. We ran up the hill and then Luke let us off the lead. We looked in bushes but Rex was not there. We looked in the river, not there. Where could he be . . .

Chapter 3 - Found him

There was one more place, on the road, there he was across the road trying to climb the tree to get the Squirrel. We told them to come home. When we got back we had dinner, laid by the fire. Soon we all fell asleep.

***Billy Evans (9)***
***Field End Junior School***

## A Day In The Life Of A Choreographer

The magpies fluttered and the crows squawked, and the noise of the annoying birds woke Sally up. A few minutes later she looked in her wardrobe for the costumes she needed for the show later on in the evening, but they were not in there. Soon she figured out that her children must have worn them to a fancy dress party, so she went downstairs and looked in the washing basket and there they were 'Oh no' thought Sally I must get these washed and dried by this afternoon. So she put them in the washing machine and then she went to the train station to catch the 1 o'clock train to Regent Street.

Once she had got to the studio she went out the back and got her unicycle. She then went out the front door to go to the audition hall. When she had got to the audition hall she went in and did the audition, it was an acting audition. After the audition there was a board that said the names of the people that had got in and at the top in big bold letters was the name Sally. She couldn't believe that she had passed. Once she had calmed down she went to the rehearsal for the show Romeo and Juliet. Of course lots of people wanted to be Juliet but it was chosen to be Sally.

It was time for the show and Sally was very nervous but the other people kept telling her there was nothing to worry about. By this time the show was about to start and already people were going on the stage. At last it was Sally's go and she was very good. At the end of the show there was a big round of applause and Sally was given some flowers.

***Lucy Wilson (8)***
***Field End Junior School***

## A Day In A Life Of A T-rex

'Long ago about 2 million years ago, there was a land long before woolly mammoths were there. The land was called The Land Of Death. It was the land of fierce T-rexs. The king T-rex was called The Death Trap King. He ruled the land and ruled other lands too. This ruler had ruled for centuries. It was a legend never to be forgotten.'

'Tell us more Grandad,' said the little girl.

The little girl was called Zelda and her cousin was called Shane.
'I'm sorry but it is your bedtime,' said Grandad.
*'Ooohh!'* said both of them.
They went into the bath and they splashed and splashed in the bathroom Soon they went to bed with a big kiss from Grandad. Then they went to bed. They both dreamed a strange dream, it was like a nightmare, a very scary nightmare.

They dreamed that they were in a very stinky dump.
'We've just had our showers,' said both of them.
'Where are we?' said Zelda.
'I don't know,' said Shane.
'I want my mummy,' said Zelda.
'Don't be such a baby for once Zelda!' said Shane.
'I'm a girl, what would you expect, a prince?' said Zelda.

'Stop arguing for once, you two!' said a voice.
'What was that voice?' said both of the children.
'Good morning you two.'
'What! Who said that? Oh it was only you Grandad.'
'Did you have a good sleep you two,' said Grandad.
*'Noooo!'* said both of them.

***Omari Elliott (9)***
***Field End Junior School***

## A DAY IN THE LIFE OF A SNEEZING PEPPER

It was a bright sunny day when the pepper was sitting on a shelf. It did a massive sneeze. It was so big that it sneezed all over the salt. The salt pushed Pepper, *Smash* the pepper went.

The salt tried to explain to everyone why Pepper was broken and why Salt was set wet. The frying pan was so grumpy that it stamped its feet.

Soon it was night-time and Salt kept dreaming about his best friend Pepper. he felt so sorry for what he done and what he had said.

When Salt woke up nobody had spoken to him but they did say, 'You're fixing Pepper back together again.'
'No I'm not.'
'Yes you are, because you broke him so you fix him,' yelled cupboard.

Salt tried the first time to fix Pepper, he fixed him and said, 'Here is Pepper!'
'No it isn't because you haven't fixed him properly and he doesn't talk.'

At last he fixed Pepper and everyone now liked Salt and they had a wonderful party.

Pepper danced with Salt and had a beautiful dance. They had wine and beer and they got very drunk Then they had dinner and five packets of crisps. It was a *brilliant party* with lots of snacks to eat and lots of chat.

***Zara Sellars (8)***
***Field End Junior School***

## A Day In The Life Of A Unicorn

As the unicorn slowly raised its head and slowly opened its eyes and looked at the sun, the unicorn stood up and walked into a meadow and ate the grass then suddenly something happened. The unicorn was lost! The mum was looking for her daughter but she couldn't find her and she took her best coat with her.

A man took the horse for a ride and the man saw her but they got away and he couldn't catch her again! The unicorn had blushing eyes but then *bang, bang, bang!*

'What's that,' said the mother. The unicorn was scared so she ran and the man couldn't find the unicorn but he found her mother. He was going to shoot the unicorn but he missed. The birds in the trees flew away because of the noise.
'The man is coming,' said the unicorn. So they ran somewhere else to hide.
'What have I done?' said the man and he ran away.
The mother and the daughter stayed where they could have some peace and quiet.

***Hannah Wood (9)***
***Field End Junior School***

## A Day In The Life Of A Grass Snake

The grass snake awoke suddenly. Where was he? This wasn't his log, it was a field. He must have sleep-slithered into the school's playing field. He tried to crawl back into the woods, but started bumping. Another knot in the tail!

The knot took ages to undo, and the snake was dozing under a tall tree. Just then a mouse ran past him. The snake uncoiled and shot after it.

The mouse was as fast as the snake, but didn't have as much sense. It thought that if it ran round a bush the snake would continue straight ahead. So, it dashed around a lavender bush, but the snake went around the lavender in the opposite direction.

It had been a very easy-to-catch breakfast. The snake was just continuing his doze when he heard screaming and shouting. There were children on a mini-beast hunt! Suddenly he heard someone shout, 'Snake!' and a girl came running towards him.

The snake disappeared into the long grass. The girl follow the snake down a muddy slope by a pond. The snake hid in the roots of a tree and . . .
*Splash*
The girl had fallen into the pond. She screamed and a panicking teacher came running to her. The teacher pulled her out of the stream, wrapped her in her coat and told the class to go. The girl was sobbing, 'Silly, silly, silly snake!'

The grass snake slithered into a garden, then into a transparent box. He fell asleep. He didn't know how long he slept, but when he awoke two boys were staring at him, and the lid was on the box. Then a voice shouted, 'Paul, Carl, lunchtime!'
'Coming!' said a boy.
They ran inside and the snake was left in the box.

The grass snake wiggled and squirmed inside the box, but he couldn't get out. Then the box tipped and toppled over! The plastic shattered, and the snake slithered away!

It wasn't evening yet, but the snake was tired. He coiled up inside a hollow log and fell asleep.

***Sophia Pope (9)***
***Field End Junior School***

## A Day In The Life Of A Teacher

My name is Mrs Billington and I am a teacher. Every day class 4B come barging into the classroom noisily as usual but when it comes to register time they all start to calm down a bit.

In the afternoons I have to shout at them because they get a bit too noisy, when they are meant to be working in complete silence. Sometimes they get annoying because I say, 'Work in silence today please!' but do they listen? No they go on chatting for the rest of the afternoon.

Next day it all starts again. This morning we are doing literacy and maths etc but in the afternoon we have got art. So when we got to the afternoon everybody got disgustingly mucky because they were making papier mâché Roman people, while I was cutting bandages and going round helping people bandage them, even I got my hands a bit dirty. The bandages had lots of powder that dropped off them. When you put them in water some of them got really soggy and horrible.

The third day we had maths and literacy. This afternoon they had to do some science. They had to see how much the temperature had gone down in exactly 12 minutes. At the end of the week I am exhausted.

***Amy Thomas (9)***
***Field End Junior School***

## A DAY IN THE LIFE OF FREDDIE

This is what happened on 12th May 1998 in the school holidays. I woke up at 12.00 midnight, it was pitch-black, the wind was howling, the curtains were blowing inside my bedroom. I crept downstairs I was looking for creatures. Mum, Dad and Laurie were so sleepy that they didn't hear me creep downstairs. I found a worm deep down in the rock-hard soil, it was sleeping too. I made a home for him then took him upstairs and switched the light off.

Next morning I woke up with a yawn, I zoomed downstairs with the worm and thought of what to call him. For twenty-four hours I clicked my fingers in the air and then I thought I'd call him Freddie.

The next day Barn Way School was open again and I ran to school, shouting, 'Bye Mum, bye Dad, bye Laurie.' I hid Freddie in the smallest pocket in my bag. I poked holes in the top so he could breath.

Mrs Disaster came over, 'Why have you got holes in your bag?'
She was from Italy. I didn't have enough time to answer before she undid my zip. I zipped up my mouth too. Freddie had hidden round the side. Freddie was my best, best friend forever.

***Sasha Nurse (9)***
***Field End Junior School***

## A Day In The Life Of A Choreographer

The crows squawked, the noise of the birds woke Sally up. A few minutes later Sally looked in her wardrobe, the costumes for the performers were gone. She figured out that her children went to a fancy dress party, they didn't have any costumes to wear. She went downstairs and there they were in a scrunched up ball in the washing machine. This added to her anger. She had breakfast and she spilled the milk everywhere. She went back upstairs to get dressed.

She walked to Uxbridge Station from Harrow. When she got to the studio she practised her part and then she did her audition. The governor told her that she had passed and she was so happy she nearly jumped out of her skin. She went backstage and got ready for the live show. She will be seen on TV and heard on the radio.

Luckily she had brought her unicycle and she rode to London Theatre on it. When she got there she went backstage and told the performers about the costumes and they went bonkers. They would have to wear what they had on, old T-shirts and baggy shorts.

When they started to argue with the choreographer she crept away to the front of the stage. She peeped through the curtains and there was the Royal Family standing by the entrance. She went backstage and sorted everything out and she told the performers that the Royal Family had been seated. They all rushed to see.

The choreographer went to get the Royal Family and to seat them comfortably. He said, 'Everybody get ready for the show, you've got five minutes. The lead star has not turned up!'

The choreographer had to call the understudy but she didn't know what to act out. The choreographer had to teach the understudy what to do. When she comes to do her part she sprains her wrist.

First Aid take her off the stage and they have to change the show to Little Red Riding Hood. At the end of the show all the cast come out and there is no applause. They go backstage and the choreograph shouts, 'I quit! Goodbye.'

***Charlotte Lawrence (9)***
***Field End Junior School***

## A Day In The Life Of A Teacher

*Chapter 1*
*Off We Go!*

Michael opened one eye and opened the other, he slid out of bed. It was 6.00am on a warm summer morning, his wife was still in bed. He ran downstairs put the kettle on, picked up his usual bowl, poured out some Cheerios, he quickly ate his breakfast and legged it back upstairs. He slammed his wardrobe open, put his favourite gear on, picked up his suitcase and ran to the car.

He got into the car, he put his keys into the car but it wouldn't start. He tried and tried but it wouldn't start so he ran to the bus station and he took the bus instead . . .

*Chapter 2*
*Oh Help!*

He finally arrived, he took the register, but Michael realised there were no helpers. He asked one of the children to get help. The children marched up the corridor to the entrance and the coach wasn't there. The child went back and said, 'Nobody will volunteer.'
Then Mrs Elliott came and said the bus had been delayed, so they all sat down and then ten minutes later the bus arrived . . .

Yeah! There were helpers on the coach. They all pushed and shoved on to the coach and it drove off. It was finally there . . .

*Chapter 3*
*Where?*

They were all having fun until something bad happened . . .

A boy got lost. Sam was his name and fun was his game. They called the locals, visitors and staff to help find him. They looked everywhere. They looked on every ride, under every bush and even down the toilet but they couldn't find him!
'I'm here, I'm here!' we could hear him crying.

*Chapter 4*
*There You Are Sam!*

The teacher turned around and Sam was there, he was so small they didn't look on the floor, they all went back to fun and laughter. They all went on the Tidal Wave . . .

Then an hour later they all went home. Mike started marking and went home, he had some Chinese dinner and stayed up till 12.00pm and went to bed.

What will happen tomorrow . . .?

***Michael Lee (8)***
***Field End Junior School***

## A Day In The Life Of A Cat

What's that noise? The radiators have come on again. Maybe I'll go upstairs . . . Creak, phew they didn't hear me. What room shall I go in. Stacey's bed is too lumpy. Tom's bed is too cold. Mum and Dad's bed is cosy, comfy, warm and perfect. So Mum's bed it is.

'Ahhh!'
'It's only the cat.'
'Chuck it out,' yelled Mum.
*Thump, thump, thump*. Dad's feet stomped down the stairs. *Bang!* The door slammed.

It's freezing out here, how would they like it. I can see a bit of light, that means it's time to explore. 'Oww, what's that? Where am I?' I think I'm in the back garden yes - yes I am in the back garden. I can hear the loud birds. 'Ahh! The bird is going for me again.' Bang, Oww I think I'm gonna have a nose-bleed. I'm gonna kill that bird.

'Cheep, cheep.'
'Where are you?'
'Cheep, cheep, cheep, cheep.'
'What's that noise.'
I know what noise that is, that's the noise for breakfast time.

Miaow, miaow, miaow.'
'Come in then.'
Miaow, miaow.'
'Here's your breakfast.'
'Cheep, cheep.'
I could still hear the bird so I forgot about my breakfast and I was ready for war.

'Cheep, cheep.' It came zooming past me. I jumped up high, got my sharp claws out and scratched it. It flew away with pain and shock. I don't think it will come back again. I enjoyed my meal without hearing the bird.

'Cheep, cheep.'
'No!'

***Emma Freebody (9)***
***Field End Junior School***

## A Day In The Life Of A Cat

I'm Julius, the super-hero-cat. I have lots of adventures, this is one of them.

I was at school in the playground when the morning bell went, it was time to go into class. I sat right at the back because I was a clever cat.

At 9.45 the fire alarm went off because there was smoke filling the lunch hall. Everyone was scared except me, but because I'm so brave I went to the hall and put the fire out myself. I suspected someone made that fire on purpose . . . This meant that we all had to go without lunch and boy was I starving!

At 3.24 the bell rang again, time to go home. I could've zoomed home; I could've jumped home; but I chose to walk home. I had a huge dinner to make up for lunch and this made me feel very tired.

At 8.45 I went to bed. When I woke up I wanted to solve the mystery of what happened yesterday at school so I went to school earlier than usual . . .

As I looked around the playground, I saw a vicious wolf dressed in black. He was pouring petrol around. I zoomed up to him and shouted, 'What are you doing!'

'I-I-I-I . . . ' the wolf stuttered, hesitated then ran off. I washed away the petrol and put a security system up that could only be operated by me. Thanks to me our school is a safer place.

***James Wolman (9)***
***Field End Junior School***

## A DAY IN THE LIFE OF AN ARTIST

Long ago was an artist called Helen. She tried to get on a plane at 9.00 am but she was stopped because it had taken off. After two hours all the birds flew away and she realised a plane had arrived. They stopped her getting on again, this was plane two, she had missed plane one. She screamed with rage.

She was tired, so she went to a hotel to spend the night. A blue jay woke her, she grumbled and left for the airport. She ran on to the plane. They took off, and she fell asleep. When she woke up some chicken was there, she hated chicken but she ate it. When she landed from America she sat down on Bournemouth beach and she started to paint. She painted a person on a body board but no-one wanted it.

She started to feel sick but she carried on painting but only one person liked her style and they bought the painting.

***Melissa Holland (9)***
***Field End Junior School***

## A Day In The Life Of Wrestler - The Rock

The Rock wakes up and worries if he's going to get badly injured. He has a healthy breakfast. He orders a Limo and tells the driver to take him straight to the stadium. He arrives at the stadium and goes into the dressing room and gets changed.

The Rock can't find his clothes. He's playing Triple H in a King of the Ring match. There's a knock on the door. It's The Undertaker and Kane they ask if he's ready. He says, 'I can't find my clothes.'
'Just put your trousers on, you'd better hurry up,' said The Undertaker.
'He's going to pay for this,' said The Rock.

Can you smell what The Rock is cooking?
Triple H was already in the ring and the bell rings and off goes Triple H and he does a pedigree. Triple H goes on the top rope and jumps but misses The Rock. The Rock gets up rock bottom. 1, 2 Triple H kicks up, it's the Dudly Boyz. They have got the table, it's 3D on Triple H. 1, 2, 3 it's all over. The Rock is the champion. Triple H is lying on the table. The Rock is the new champion. It's the Dudly Boyz they have put Triple H in the dustbin. Oh no! He goes flying off the stage and it's all over.

***Mauro Urgo (9)***
***Field End Junior School***

# A Day In The Life Of A Horse And Horse Rider

In Ruislip in Fore Street two miles ahead are Jack's stables. Where Johnny, Emma, Ashley Angie and Michelle are getting up on their horses.
'Are we all buckled up?' Emma said.
'Yes,' everyone said.
So out they went into the wood.
'So where are we going?' asked Michelle.
'We will go to the sand track,' shouted Emma.
So off they went.
'Let's start trotting because we only have a hour until we have to be back,' said Emma.

All of a sudden Ebony, who Johnny was riding started to trot back. So Emma went after him. Then Ebony started to canter back. A few minutes later she couldn't see him. So she decided to go to the stables. When she got there she found Ebony eating hay. She quickly put the lead reign on him and very quickly they caught up with the others.

They then got to the sand track and had a nice canter and gallop and then headed back to the stables to feed the horses and then go home.
Before they went home they booked for the next week. They went home and had a bite to eat and then went to the Cricket Club for an hour and then went back home to sleep .

***Nik Mills (9)***
***Field End Junior School***

## A Day In The Life Of A Teddy Bear Called Patch

In a toy shop, on a shelf was a teddy bear with an eye patch. He had been there for a very long time because nobody wanted him until one day when a little four year-old girl called Hannah saw him. She bought him and loved him loads and always played with him.

Soon it was Hannah's birthday. She got lots and lots of presents but her favourite one was a teddy that walked and talked by itself. She soon started to forget about Patch. Later Patch woke and found himself in the road. All the other toys, a Barbie doll, Buster a dog, Trotters a pig and Stompers an elephant noticed Patch was gone.

They looked out of the window and saw Patch lying there in the road.
'He's in trouble,' Stompers said. 'We better help him before another car goes over him.'
All the toys tied six of Hannah's skipping ropes together and threw the rope out of the window.
'Hold on to this!' Buster shouted to Patch.
He did. They pulled and pulled and then they finally pulled him up.

Later Hannah's mum came into Hannah's room and saw how dirty Patch was. 'I better clean you up,' she said.
After she did that, Hannah came upstairs crying, 'My teddy is broken!'
'No it's probably just run out of batteries,' her mum told her. 'Play with Patch instead while I try to buy you new batteries.'
Hannah did.

In a few days her mum forgot about getting new batteries and so Hannah always played with Patch.

***Hayley Marr (9)***
***Field End Junior School***

## A Day In The Life Of The Escape

'Mum, I'm just going to say goodnight to Sparkles and Nibbles, then go to bed. OK!' Rachel was about to go bed so she said goodnight to the hamsters and went to bed. She forgot to close Nibbles' cage. Nibbles climbed out and opened Sparkles' cage.

They climbed into the ball and rolled to the bird cage. The hamsters clung on to a piece of thread that Rachel left earlier. They climbed till they reached the bird cage and opened the door. The bird flew out of the cage and got a bag. What the bird was going to do was carry the hamsters in the bag around the house. So the bird told them what he was going to do and the hamsters agreed. So they got in the bag and the bird picked the bag up and flew to the corner.

In the corner was a big spider that was pulling faces at them. The bird nipped at his legs and the hamsters tried to fight with him. In the end the hamsters won. So the hamsters got in the bag and the bird took them upstairs.

Upstairs was a cat. The cat ran into the bag and the bird flew away. The cat wasn't looking where he was going and fell down the stairs with a bang and woke the people up. They went to the cage and closed the door.

***Rachel Lehane (9)***
***Field End Junior School***

## A Day In The Life Of A Magic Cuddly Toy

One hot sunny, lovely day a boy called Bob went to a shop and brought a cuddly toy for his sister called Tina. He didn't know it but it was a magical toy. He took it home and when Tina touched it, she called for help.

Today she cried to Bob, 'My cuddly toy is lost but I will find out where it is.'
Bob shouted to her, 'You do not know where to start.'
'You're right.'
'Hang on I think I know who stole your cuddly toy, it was the bad boy with the dog. When he touched it he and his dog got smaller.'
Tina said, 'That will teach him a lesson.'
She got her cuddly toy back and the boy and his dog did not turn back to their normal size.

Tina could do magic so she got her other cuddly toys down and all had a magic tea party. She had more money so she bought some more cuddly toys. She went upstairs but her bedroom was a mess, so her cuddly toys and Tina did some magic and her bedroom was tidy now. Her cuddly toys were reading Harry Potter Book 3. She cried out to Bob, 'That's funny they are reading my Harry Potter book.'
Her cuddly toys were angry with her. Now she was a doll and she couldn't get back to normal.

Bob and Tina clicked their fingers and spoke and Tina was a girl again. So they lived happily with their mum and dad.

***Rebecca Lanning (9)***
***Field End Junior School***

## A Day In The Life Of Four Friends

Tom, Anthony, Matthew and Thomas were friends. They were walking along a high and rocky cliff on a hike to Mount Eagle. Anthony kept saying, 'Are we there yet?'
'Another couple of miles,' Tom replied.

Finally they reached Mount Eagle, so they did what they came to do . . . watch the eagles!

Tom and Anthony hadn't read their hiking manuals but the other two had. Tom and his friend were so eager to see the birds they got too close, they got careless and fell off into the water below.

Brave Thomas and Matthew abseiled down but couldn't find them anywhere. Whilst Thomas and Matthew were looking for their friends, Tom and Anthony had managed to find a snowy cave to rest in. Unfortunately a wampa lived there too! A wampa is a big scary white creature with a fanged mouth.

Anthony and his friend struggled and struggled but couldn't get free of the wampa. Then Tom remembered he had his light sabre (and for those who don't know what a light sabre is, it is a sword of sorts) and he used it to protect them both. They managed to run outside but the wampa tried to grab them.

Just then a massive eagle swooped down and saved them, it brought the two boys up the cliff, where they were reunited with the others.

Tom and Anthony thanked the eagle and went home. They checked their manuals and found it said, 'Rule No 501, Don't go near a cliff edge!' It didn't mention the white wampas!

***Tom King (9)***
***Field End Junior School***

## A Day In The Life Of A Holiday Rabbit

On a beautiful summer's day a little girl and her mum went to a pet shop. At the very back of the pet shop there were rabbits, one of the rabbits that Sally saw was two years old, he had been at that pet shop for his whole life.
'I want this one,' Sally said, proudly pointing at the two year-old rabbit.
'Sally, darling that's three pounds. I'm not spending that kind of money on a rabbit,' her mum said annoyed.
'I don't care how much it is, I want it and I want it now!' Sally shouted at the top of her voice.
'Okay,' her mum said embarrassed.

When they got home they put the rabbit in its new hutch. Later when Sally went to stroke Beauty, she opened the cage and touched him and the next thing she realised was she was in Morocco. She turned around and Beauty ran off to another rabbit called Brandy.

They had spent an hour in Morocco having drinks and playing lots of games. 'This is the best holiday ever,' she said in an exited voice.
They walked around for ages then she looked at her watch, she gasped, 'It's 12 o'clock and I have school.' Then she touched Beauty and then she was back home. Sally loved the free holiday but she had to rush after school and do the work she missed.

Sally had enough but then she thought, 'Why don't I go in the evening and I'll have nothing to worry about!'

***Rhoswyn Heale (9)***
***Field End Junior School***

## A Day In The Life Of A Time Capsule

Dear reader,

Today I'm going to tell you a story about a boy and a girl, their names are Maisie and Harry. Maisie is the eldest, for she is 13 and Harry, he's only 6.

Now, here is the hero of the story. It was an ordinary Saturday morning in Maisie's house as her and her brother had just finished a nice bowl of Kellogg's cornflakes with semi-skimmed milk. Maisie was getting ready to go down to the local newsagents called Stars.

But on the way she stopped and thought, what's that? It was a thin and narrow box over the road. It was a time capsule. The next thing I knew was, she was dancing in Jamaica, dancing and dancing. Then said her goodbyes. Next stop was space. When she got there she met lots of aliens - green ones and brown ones. Soon she whispered sleepily ' I have to go, bye.'

Her next journey was to Stars. She got a nice box of Celebrations, yum yum and then travelled home.

When Maisie got back she told the story to Harry.
'Can I come?' he said.
'Maybe next time,' Maisie said. 'It's eight o'clock already.'

Next thing there was a beaming light and her alien friends had come back, then smoke came and took them back where they belonged. Now you know Maisie and Harry.

***Katie Fulbrook (9)***
***Field End Junior School***

## A Day In The Life Of A Land Of Chocolate

At Easter, I got a huge Easter egg. I could just about fit inside it. Inside was a note, I read it out, it said:

> 'Yum, you
> Delicious block
> Take me to the land
> Of choc!'

Suddenly I was in a strange world where everywhere I could smell chocolate. It was a dream come true. I walked around and found a tree with Rolos hanging from the dark brown branches. I picked one and out popped two legs and then two arms . . .
'Hello Ciara.'
'H . . . h . . . how do you know my name?' I mumbled.
'Oh never mind that,' the Rolo replied, 'I just want to welcome you to Chocoland.'
'Oh thank you, but would you mind showing me around?'

So Mr Rolo showed me a lake made of Nesquick milkshake. I picked one of the daffodil cups and filled it with milkshake.

Mr Rolo needed a rest. While he slept I had a sneak inside the chocolate factory, not heeding the sign saying: *Do not go in or else!*

I saw all the new inventions like Funky-Fiz. As I was walking I turned brown. I licked myself. I discovered that I had turned chocolate. Oh no, it's probably a spell. I need to get back home.

I thought and thought until . . .

Of course, the spell that I said to get here! I said it, it didn't work. I tried to think of another spell:

'Err you
Disgusting block
Take me to the land
Of rock.'

Bang! I was home. Wait a minute, where's my Easter egg?
'Nooo! Don't eat it Lucy!'

***Chelsey Costello (9)***
***Field End Junior School***

## A Day In The Life Of My Dog

My day normally starts when I get up and go upstairs to wake everyone up by jumping on their beds. Then they let me out in the garden for a bit, while they get my breakfast ready, hopefully it's something nice like sausages. On this particular day it was boring dog food which I have nearly every day. After breakfast they went upstairs to get dressed.

Finally Richard and Thomas took me to Ruislip Lido which is one of my best places to go for a walk and swim. When we got there I chased some swans and had a swim. Richard and Thomas then took me for a walk in the woods. When we were in the middle I started to chase a squirrel, I ran and ran but then I tripped over. It really hurt and I barked and barked. Richard picked me up and had to carry me for about two miles. He had to keep on putting me back onto the ground to have a rest. After a while someone helped Richard and they took me to my worst place in the world - *the vets!*

When we went in I think the vet said I had a broken tendon so he gave me a horrible injection. I had an operation and had my leg stitched up, I then went home to have a nice long sleep.

***Thomas Clissold (9)***
***Field End Junior School***

## A Day In The Life Of My Rabbit

'Hayley, come down here!' I shouted.
'What!'
'Fudge is magic!' She came running downstairs.
'Look he can talk.'
'Hello,' Fudge screamed, thinking we couldn't hear.

My sister couldn't believe her *own* eyes, on the other hand Fudge was just staring in the distance. We went out to get some shopping - carrots, cabbage leaves, special chocolate buttons and normal cabbage. When we came back he wasn't in his cage! We went to Covent Garden in London and went to the tramp houses. We knocked on all the doors except one, it was our only hope!
'Come on, we've got to try,' Hayley said.
'We've been walking for hours!' I puffed. We knocked, Fudge came running to the door.
'Get me out, get me out!' he shouted.
'Open the door with your excellent magic.'
So he did, we ran with the tramp not knowing.
'Are you OK?'
'Just about,' he said.

We got back home, we got him his food from the fridge. 'Fudge make the police arrest him,' I said.
'OK, it's done.'
'That was quickly done.'
'That's my magic,' then he was eating.
'Yes it is!'
'Don't talk when eating,' I said furiously. 'I can't believe that tramp would take you away,' I said with sympathy.
'Shows how nice I am?'

***Emily Begner (9)***
***Field End Junior School***

## A Day In The Life Of A Fish

Dear diary,

It all happened so fast. One minute I'm swimming in the sea with legs and arms, the next I am still swimming in the sea but I was a fish.

Under the water I saw sights I had never seen before. Beautiful corals and colours and fish. I swam deeper and further in the ocean and then I saw it - a fish's dreaded enemy, a shark was heading right towards me. Fish scattered in all directions, I saw some helpless fish being swallowed up. At that instant I realised that I'd have to think of a plan if I was going to survive. It was hard because I had to swim and think at the same time. So, it wasn't a complicated plan but if I could lose the swarm of fish I would have to do it there and then. I headed for the edge of the swarm and then when I was near some coral I darted into it and hid. It worked, the shark swam straight past me. I saw a beautiful creature so I said 'Hello,' but he was not friendly. He said that he would eat me if I didn't leave him alone so off I swam again. Shallower and shallower it became until I got to the shore. I hit a person's leg and then there was sparks of magic and puffs of smoke and I was a human again.

Anyway, that was my day in the life of a fish, bye.

***Kelly Smith (10)***
***Field End Junior School***

## A Day In The Life Of A Fox

I am a fox cub and this is my tale:

I was sitting waiting for my mother to return from her hunting expedition, suddenly she ran in and growled, 'Out the back exit, hunters coming fast.'

I stood rooted to the spot for three minutes then I heard a faint barking getting closer. I scrambled up to the tunnel. I ran and as I stopped I noticed my mum wasn't with me. I ran back and she was lying motionless with a bullet in her head. A rustle in the bushes behind me, made me turn. Behind me was the father I'd never seen once. He murmured 'Run as fast as your paws can carry you, they are coming go to the forest and to human Sally who saved you from the wolf, I'll come until Owl's Tree.' I ran and as I got to Owl's Tree I could still hear the hunt cry and smell humans.

I went to Sally and she said 'Shoo, you are well.' Then she heard the cry of the hounds. I sneaked in and Sally gave me some milk. I was tucked up in bed with a blanket around me. I looked like a cat. Someone pounded on the door. I was shaking. The pounding stopped and footsteps faded away. I lay and cried for my *slaughtered* mother.

***Hayley Kennedy (10)***
***Field End Junior School***

## A Day In The Life Of A Rabbit

'Phew, it's hot,' I said lying down, 'there's no shade, all sun. Oh a person is coming. What's she got in her hand? She's coming closer. It's a piece of cloth with a strawberry on it!'

I closed my eyes. I felt a nudge. It was Mum.
'There's no sun. It's gone all dark. She put the tea towel on our cage.' I said to myself.
*'Mum! Mum!'* She had turned over, that is what the nudge was.
'What darling?'
'There's no sun, all shade. What's happened?'
'It's all right. Mrs Pinkstar has put a tea towel over us to cool us. You don't need to have a heart attack!' she said not worried.
'Why can't we take our coats off?' I wondered biting my spotty black and white fur. 'Mum, Mum wake up!'
'What is it now?'
'Why can't we take our coats off?'
'Because Glitter, it's stuck,' she said stuttering.
*'Stuck! Stuck!'*
'Yes stuck.'
'But Mrs Pinkstar's coat isn't stuck,' I said.
'Well yes.'
'So!'
'Hers is made by factory people.'

She came out and put us on a lead.
'Where are we going?'

She took us down the pet shop, at that moment a nasty looking man took us home!

***Amanda Bonnar (10)***
***Field End Junior School***

## A Day In The Life Of A Human

It was my first day at school. I wasn't very scared when I got in the playground. My mum kissed me and left me. I didn't know what to do. I walked over to a lonely boy and said 'Hi,' then the whistle blew and we went in. I really wanted to make friends with him.

First we met our teacher, she told us to write down on a piece of paper what we would like. We had two lessons and then we went to play. I saw the boy and said 'Do you want to be friends?'
He said 'OK.'

A boy came past and called him Midget and I said 'Stop that.' He kicked my friend. I told the teacher.
She said 'Stay away from that boy,' which wasn't much help. Me and the boy walked off feeling angry. We played cops and robbers but that got boring. I said 'Do you want to play?'
He said 'I can't run.'

The bell went, we did science and literacy, then I invited the boy to my house. He said he'd come round. My mum asked who was he and I said that he was my new friend.
'What you want for dinner?' she asked.
'Chicken nuggets and chips,' we said.

When we went outside we played cricket then he went home. When I went to school we got changed for PE. I looked at my friend, he had no toes.

***Dominic Brall (10)***
***Field End Junior School***

## A Day In The Life Of My Cousin's Rabbit

'Wow, I'm getting a real treat today, I'm going to my auntie's house,' said Jasmin to her stuffed toy.
'We're here. I can't wait for some dandelions, carrots and luxury rabbit food.'
'Hello Sarah, how's Jasmin?' asked April.
'She's all right thanks,' replied Sarah.
'Bye Sarah,' called Jasmin, 'I think I'll go exploring in the garage.'

When she got into the garage she said, 'Hello, who are you?'
'I'm Darren, April's rabbit, who are you?'
'I'm Jasmin, Sarah's pet.'
'April hides our food all around the garden and house for us to find.'
'Where's my bed?'
'It's over here.'
'Thank you.'
'That's OK.'
'Are you hungry or thirsty?'
'Yes, sort of. It was a long journey.'
'Well, if you come with me I'll find some food, what do you like?'
'My favourite is carrots and watery milk.'
'I'll show you where they all are. The dandelions are picked and are on the grass, the carrots are on the flowers and finally the rabbit food is in the tray. You walk in one end, eat out of the other for food, but for water you do the same but in the other tray'
'Thanks.'
'Oh and the toys are here.'
'Do you want a game of pogodo?'
'That will be great.'

They played a game of pogodo and then they went for some food and drink, then went to sleep.

Five years later April adopted Jasmin. Darren and Jasmin got married. They had thirty baby rabbits.

***Samantha Jones (9)***
***Field End Junior School***

## A Day In The Life Of A Coach

We were on our way to the coach, people getting on and people getting off. That's the day in the life of a coach. It's jump and run all over the place, everywhere children swap seats. Up steep mountains and down steep hills, over the bumps and up the ramps, chugging along the roads really slowly, round the roundabouts as we go all the cars go round real slow.

The lights flash really brightly and they always make me crash, the people jump and fall backwards and jerk forwards. My engine's burnt and it's dehydrated. I let out a burp of heat and suddenly skidded onto my side. People inside me cried and cried for their loved ones by their side.

The ambulance came really fast and said to my driver I might not last. The children were rescued and taken away and on my side, there I lay. Windows broken, wheels in the air, people staring everywhere. Everybody says 'It's time to go home,' but they are walking away with a groan. The coach was tired and falling asleep. 'When will they get me back on my feet? Come quickly and take me away, I've had a most distressing day.'

***Sarah Chisholm (10)***
***Longfield Middle School***

## Ratty The Toy Rat's Day

Hi my name is Ratty,
My friends think I'm batty.
The life of a cuddly toy,
Is a thing that I enjoy.
The love of my owner,
Makes me nothing but a loner.
I'm tattered and torn,
I've been thrown on the lawn.
My eye's coming of,
And I'm getting a cough.
I get taken for walks
And my mum talks.
I sit by the window every night,
Sitting, waiting, waiting for light.
The beautiful dawn,
The new bird's born.
My life's a rush
And I need a brush.
Dew outside,
I had a ride,
From the local bus,
So there is no fuss.
We went to the zoo
And all the penguins said 'Coo.'
It rained and rained
And that cough I gained.
We went home
And sat in the tent dome.
My head was wrapped up
And I was sick in a cup.
Down the night fell
And the baby started to yell.
The stars shone brightly
And mummy snored lightly.

Out the window bats flew
And the owls said 'Tu-whit tu-whoo.'
Up comes the sun,
My life has begun.
The beautiful rise,
Would win first prize.
Red, yellow, orange and blue
And the birds said 'Coo.'
The new day has come
And I have a hungry tum!

***Kelly Hoskins (10)***
***Longfield Middle School***

## A DAY IN THE LIFE OF A TEDDY BEAR

I look up at the sky at night
There I see stars shining bright
Above the Earth the glowing moon
I hope I will go and visit it soon.

I walk along the dirt track road
Wondering if the stars make a code
I love the moon and shining stars
But I definitely hate noisy cars.

The dropping moon, the rising sun
I love this time, it's good for fun
Time for games with other bears
Snakes and ladders, truths and dares.

Now the sun is rising fast
No one wants to be the last
To run and hide from humans
Us teddy bears show off our acumens.

I watch from my hiding place
The humans run a shocking race
Then a baby comes into sight
Licks me on the nose, what a fright!

Then the humans walk away
On this very hot day in May
Out of my hiding place I scuttle
I hear a bear's little chuckle.

I hear other bears laugh too
I wander off to join their crew
Holly, Calim, Sal and Sam
Bill, Strawberry and Raspberry jam.

My new friends' names
New bears to play games
With these new friends of mine
I feel really, really, really, really fine.

***Amy Tribbick (10)***
***Longfield Middle School***

## A DAY IN THE LIFE OF THE SEA

As I awaken the sun shines upon my body, the fish glide through my waters and the gulls soar through the sky. As the day gets hotter, humans bathe upon the golden, sparkling sand, children swimming, shouting, playing. Dolphins play in the shallow water, gently squeaking, you can hear them from the heavens. But suddenly it starts to rain, my children fall from the skies, people run to take shelter, some scream. Lightning strikes, thunder roars like a lion, children cry, parents try to comfort them.

The rain stops and the scared sun comes out of hiding from behind the clouds. The children stop crying and run back into me, no longer afraid. Far, far away a baby dolphin is born and swims to the surface to have its first breath of air. It swims back to its mother, its fragile flippers flapping up and down, darting here and there. At the same time a baby seagull is born on a cliff. As the egg hatches, the baby gull chirps for food. The mother flaps its gentle wings as it flies over the water. It catches a fish and takes it back to its child. Lots of things happen in my life, I am important.

***Nicholas Todd (10)***
***Longfield Middle School***

## A Day In The Life Of An Australian Bush

It's lovely to be an Australian bush. You get an amazing view of sunrise, a bright, glowing orange ball with fairies leaving pink and red trails through the sky. It's wonderful to hear a kookaburra's lullaby as the morning goes on. It's extremely relaxing to have a massage by the beautiful brumbies' hooves as they gallop off to green pastures around lunch time. Their gentle mouths pulling up the grass tickles immensely and the wind caused by their swishing tails keeps me cool. Many scaly lizards scuttle across my face at the hottest point of the day.

As it cools down, I love to watch the golden coloured dingoes, the leopards of Australia, play in the shade pouncing and prancing over my stomach, which gives me tummy ache. When their mother comes back, dragging along a hare dripping blood onto my face like ink, they rush off to meet her. As a dark blanket, known as night, is draped across the sky I stare at the large, twinkling fireflies, then I silently fall asleep.

***Hollie Glazebrook (10)***
***Longfield Middle School***

## A Day In The Life Of An Alien

I wander around baffled, not knowing where I am. I don't know what happened, all I can remember is that I was dropped down from a huge galaxy, Zindri. Suddenly I see some sort of weird creature. I check on my electronic device and it says 'human.' Human is a living thing from Earth. It reproduces, grows, talks and moves. I look astonished. Wow, what a thing. No, I'm on Earth.

Now all I can see is this big blue thing above and weird green things with food on them. Also, some sort of transport with wheels on it. I have a really strange feeling about this. I think, 'Wow, this is Earth.' I look around with humans staring at me saying, 'Alien.' Wow, I know I am. As I look around, I see some bags with things on them and humans are holding them. I ask one of the humans where I can stay.
'Um, let's see, a house, hotel or a flat.'
'Where can I get one of these things?'
'Well, you can go to a hotel up on the hill and flats are in this building,' the human said. 'Mr, you're really freaky.'
As I go on my journey to find a hotel, I see a sign and I go in. Then suddenly, everything starts to shake rapidly. I fall from one side to another. After, everyone freezes and then everything goes pitch black. Suddenly, a huge alien with long stripes of snake for hair, eyes the size of a door, mouth as big as a sea and huge ears the size of a hurricane, appears. 'Who are you?'
'I am the god of all aliens and I have come to say that you are going back to Zindri, your home.'
'What happened and how do you know?' I said.
'It doesn't matter. Now you are coming with me to the galaxy Zindri.'
In a flash I went up to space.

***Shefali Shah (10)***
***Longfield Middle School***

## A Day In The Life Of A Football Player

The twenty players on the pitch are all running for the ball, trying to score. The other two are goalkeepers waiting for the ball to come. The audience is watching the ball go from side to side, cheering for their team. Who knows who is going to win?

Ten minutes until the match finishes, players sweating. Audience shouting and cheering more and more every minute for their team. Babies crying hungrily and tired, wanting the match to finish. Who knows who is going to win?

A penalty for a team, will they score or not? The ball goes in and the player scores. All the players run up to their team-mates, happy as you've never seen them before. Now the score's 1-1. Who knows who is going to win?

Five minutes to play, tension's mounting. Everybody's quiet now, the players are taking it easy. Who knows who is going to win?

Somebody's injured, so the team physio comes out and takes him away to check if he is all right, but no, he is not, so a sub comes out and plays for him. But he is not that good, he gets a yellow card straight away. Who knows who is going to win?

It is injury time now, the score's 1-1, there are ten seconds to play. Is anyone going to score? The whistle goes, the match has finished, the score at the end is 1-1. They tried very, very hard.

***Priya Raja (10)***
***Longfield Middle School***

## The Life Of An Eagle

I am an eagle
Living alone
I'm just a bird
Sitting on my throne.

I live the simple way of life
Sitting on my nest
Until the time for eating comes
When my stomach rumbles best.

Nine to five my working day
I swoop down to catch my prey
Returning to my nest I lay
An egg that looks so big and grey.

Welcome to the world I say
Then the egg begins to crack
First appears his tiny head
And then his feeble back.

I stroke his feathers lovingly,
Encourage him to stand and fly
I look to him for gratitude
But all that he can do is cry.

His hunger drives me off for prey
And gaining speed every second
I spot my target down below
Where into my eagle eyes he beckoned.

I see the detail on his wings
And his tiny feathers
Now I am close enough to touch
They feel like shammy leathers.

I bite his tail with my teeth
Down to the ground he fell
Just like a brown autumn leaf
How far he fell I cannot tell.

But down I swoop to fetch him
He is dead with a broken limb
I lift him up with my beak
As the light grows dim.

I fly for home, him on my shoulder
A job well done
A satisfactory victory
Now feeding time has come.

***Christopher Henson (10)***
***Longfield Middle School***

## A Day In The Life Of A Theme Park

As the morning starts, the rides get checked and slowly the park opens. People swarm in like a bunch of hungry lions. People frantically queue. Finally, the carriage of the roller-coaster starts to move and then music starts. Food is sold, people rage to get on a ride. Banana boat swings, you can hear the ghost house roar. Game stalls getting more than enough customers. The day brightens and more people pile in. The water rides soak, people laugh.

Suddenly, the roller-coaster stops. People cry a sound of terror. The ride has broken down. Bumper cars crash, people angry in a happy way. As the time strikes 5pm, the lights dim, but the fairground lights brighten. Little children leave, big teenagers come, they ride on things that terrify some people. Finally, late at night, the park is closed for another day. As the morning starts, the rides get checked and slowly . . .

***Robert Brown (10)***
***Longfield Middle School***

## BRUNO THE BULLDOG

As I slowly wake, I shake as I slowly walk to my water bowl. I slurp and I burp from my water bowl. I am a cute little bulldog, always eating, sleeping, drinking, playing with my owners. I live peacefully at home.

Every day I get two walks. I go running in the fields and I get a nice treat. I love to run, jump and leap while my owners are chasing me round and round a tree. With glee I run and jump in muddy puddles. When I get home, they give me a nice bubble bath, where they wash me to get all the mud off.

Then I go to my basket and I drop down asleep while the sun is hiding.

***John Vinton (10)***
***Longfield Middle School***

## A Tree

Morning: High in the sky the sun comes up, it's like a day waking up. This time I'm a tree of faith and things are looking very good around me as my leaves turn to the sun as it comes out.

Lunch time: The river branches. My roots take the water that takes the food that is put through and goes round.

Afternoon: Kids are climbing on me. My branches fall down, but grow again. School is done. More kids are rushing through me. My leaves shake as their hats and bodies go past me.

Night-time: Night-time falls upon me as the sun goes down and shadows loom around me.

***Anish Bhagat (10)***
***Longfield Middle School***

## A Day In The Life Of A Chameleon

Hi, I'm a chameleon and I live in Africa and Madagascar. I live in rainforests, jungles and tropical forests. I can see very well and I can move my eyes all the way around to see everything. I have huge eyes. To lay my eggs I come down from the tree and lay them in a mouldy old bush. In a few weeks, I check to see if my babies have hatched. When my beautiful babies have hatched, I put them on my head and take them up a tree. I eat my favourite insects for my breakfast. I eat flies, crickets and bugs, yummy, yummy. My favourite meal is a big, fat, juicy locust. I eat one meal a day and then I rest up in my tree for the rest of the day to digest my food, then go to sleep. My horrible enemies are birds. Normally, but chameleons like me will hardly ever attack the little chameleons unless they're very hungry. We special green chameleons grow up to 12.7cm long. Jackson chameleons grow up to 63cm long, that's quite big. They come from Africa.

All chameleons have great camouflaged bodies against branches and trees. We're the world's greatest camouflage experts (wow). My incubation lasted three months. It went really quickly. When my babies hatch out of their eggs, they become lovely baby chameleons. Dwarf brookesias can balance on a human's little finger.

***April Sullivan (9)***
***Longfield Middle School***

## A Day In The Life Of A Soldier

My name is Sir Roger Walton and I am in the army. I have to go to war and it is a really tough job. I do a lot of training because I need to be strong, balanced and fast. I have to be strong because I need to carry heavy things. I have to be balanced so I can cross a thin rope bridge and I have to be fast so I can run away from someone.

In the morning, I get up out of my comfy tent at 5am. Because I am high up in the army, someone makes my breakfast, which is sausages, baked beans, fried egg and bacon. After breakfast, I have shooting practice with my gun. I need to practise with a bazooka because I am not very good at it.

After shooting practise it is time for lunch. After lunch, we have to do more training. This time it is running and over an assault course. This is very hard work and we usually get very dirty because we have to crawl through the mud and water.

In the evening, I have a nice meal and then go to bed in my comfy tent. I hope we don't have to go to war again, because the last time, my best friend nearly died when a German sniper shot him.

***Nicholas Margalski (10)***
***Longfield Middle School***

## A Day In The Life Of A Polar Bear

I love being a polar bear, but one thing that I do not like is the weather because it is too cold, but to help me is my fur coat. My fur has a coat of black, then on top is white. My food is lovely. The food I eat is seals and walrus. I had a seal for breakfast just this morning. I don't like the tourists that visit us because they litter the environment and also kill some of the polar bear family for our fur. We have no chance of living with hunters killing us.

I enjoy swimming with my friends and we go hunting for food. I am going to have cubs today. I will need to help my cubs learn to swim and hunt for their food. In the future, they will live on their own.

My cubs are born and I have to teach them how to swim.

It is a year later and now my cubs are very good swimmers. They hunt for food for me so that I do not have to work, but I do go swimming sometimes. Soon I will be a grandmother. My big girl is going to have a cub and I am so excited. When the cub is born, I am going to teach him as well.

***Pavetha Seeva (9)***
***Longfield Middle School***

## A Day In The Life Of Sachin Tendulkar

I'm Sachin Tendulkar, a famous cricket player. I play for my country, India. I became a cricketer by starting my training and working hard at a very young age. My career as a cricketer has given me good money and fame. It's really fun playing cricket. I've hit a lot of centuries and half centuries in test match and one-day series. I was chosen as Sports Icon of the Century, it made me very happy and I was proud of myself then.

I'm not a very good bowler. Once I bowled an over when I played against Australia and it was a very successful over. I got a wicket and only gave them one run, but my second over wasn't very successful. At the end of the test match, my team lost but we enjoyed playing the match.

I have played many tournaments like the Sharjah, the World Cup and quite a lot of tri-series. Our first cup we won was the Sharjah Cup. At that time I was not in the team. India played really well and was very happy.

I'm quite good at fielding. I like catching the ball, so most of the time I'm a slip-fielder, which is about one metre behind the wicket keeper and ready for the catches. I also lead my team as a captain at times.

I like playing for India and my team. I'm proud to be an Indian and to play for India.

***Rushil Vithlani (9)***
***Longfield Middle School***

## A Day In The Life Of A Dog

Hello! My name is Amica, I'm a dog. I'm not really a dog though, but Megan is! She's my owner for today you see, and I'm her dog. I suppose it's all right being a dog, but I'm not so keen on the food. Megan gave me rabbit and as I was so hungry, I gobbled it all up and now my throat hurts. Anyway, right now I'm hiding in the mulberry bush because Megan is trying to groom me. I know you want to know what grooming is, well it's when a great big brush runs down your back and really hurts. Now you'll be wondering how do I know, well it's because Megan tried to groom me earlier on in the day.

Uh oh, here's Megan. She's come into the garden. 'Amica, where are you?' Oh here goes, I'm going to flee. I'll run into the lounge. Oh look, 'Diggit's' on the TV and oh, Jasper, he's so cute. Oh how nice, ugh, ouch, I don't care. Oh look, my rag, Megan's got it. I'm going to get it and then run off upstairs. Here goes, I've got it now. I'll go upstairs. Oh, I've just remembered it's dinner time. Yum, yum, yum. What a way to end the day. A massage from Megan and my favourite dog food, not forgetting I get to change back to a human and Megan back to a dog.

***Roma Tournier-Blake (8)***
***Longfield Middle School***

## A Day In The Life Of A Slave

I'm a slave. My parents died when I was little. I haven't got a job or any money. Some things I can't afford. At the moment I live with a rich family, but even though they are rich, they don't give me a proper place to sleep or proper food to eat. It's just not fair. I feel so awful and tired. I'm so sleepy. That family shouts so much, even if they are little. I sleep on a dirty bed and it's so hard, I wish my family was here. That family says 'Slave, come here. Do this, do that.' I'm sick and tired, I must do something. This boy called Tom gets on my nerves. My parents used to say I should work hard. I never used to work hard and look at me. I'm a slave. Why are parents right all the time? It's my bedtime.

The next morning it's like it always is. I feel like I'm cracked in pieces. I just don't know. I can't stand it anymore. I'm going somewhere else. I don't want to live in this stupid place. My clothes are cut in pieces and my shoes, they are broken. I feel so bored.

***Saher Gardezi (9)***
***Longfield Middle School***

## A Day In The Life Of A Koala

Hi, I am a koala. I have a lovely life, eating and sleeping all day! I look after my babies who hang on to my back and it gives me a backache, but I make up for it by eating lots of yummy eucalyptus leaves. I live in a special place where I am taken care of by some lovely people who look after us and the other animals who live here. The girls get us out of our cages and the boys feed us. The girls' names are Rebecca, Laura and Roma. The boys' names are Richard, Gary and Daniel. They are all very nice people, I would like to stay here for the rest of my life.

I was bought here when there had been a terrible fire in my forest. I do not know where my mummy is, but I still think of her and wish she could see my babies. She was a very nice mummy. I did not know my dad, I still think of my family a lot, but at least I am safe now and my babies will be safe too. Becca (short for Rebecca) is a girl who takes the babies out to play during the day. They are often too tired to play for long, but they do like Becca and look forward to seeing her each day. Gary is the boy who feeds us, so we all like him.

***Laura Bodimeade (9)***
***Longfield Middle School***

## A Day In The Life Of A Tiger

I am Sabrina the tiger, I am only a cub. I always think of meat. I wish I could hunt like my mum and my dad. I Live in a jungle, a big one. I really like it here. I have some friends, like Mike who's a lion cub and Jess the squirrel and lots more. I always like to jump and play. My mum and dad say I talk too much. Every day when I get hungry, my dad goes hunting and when he comes back, my mum cuts little chunks of meat for me. I like being a cub because I always get what I want. Oh I love it, being a cub. I am scared of the dark because we live in a dark place, the jungle. You know how being a cub is really fun and joyful! My mum and dad are very kind, they buy me a lot of toys.

I love my mum and my dad because they always remember my birthday. My birthday is today, I just remembered. Oh gosh! Everyone remembered my birthday and the presents I wanted. This is the best party ever.

Yesterday was fun and I am really tired today. Oh yeah! I am ten weeks old and I know my own language. You see I always think of playing. I wish I could write but I can't, because I've got paws not fingers. Any way, I can hear my parent calling me. Bye, bye.

***Neima Said (9)***
***Longfield Middle School***

## A Day In The Life Of A Squirrel

Hello! I am a squirrel who lives in a tree in the forest and I eat acorns. I have a bushy tail. I wonder if any other animal lives in a tree in the forest? In the autumn I search around the forest for acorns and I put them in my home, so when winter comes I will have enough food to eat. I am comfortable sleeping in my warm house. I do like listening to the rustling of the leaves. I am good at climbing trees. Oh, I almost forgot, my name is Mr Squirrel. I love combing trees. I don't think it's fun in winter, I have to stay in my home all day long. Boring.

I love playing with my friends near my home. One of my friends is really naughty and annoys me. He is called Mr Rat. I do like him a bit. My best friend is called Mr Rabbit. It's almost past my bedtime. I do like Miss Squirrel. Oh no! I left my washing outside and it's starting to rain! My best friend Mr Rabbit's T-shirt is out there! Miss Squirrel's beautiful party dress is out there! What shall I do? I know I could go out and get them in, but I am so tired. Never mind, goodnight!

*Nicole Gibbs (9)*
***Longfield Middle School***

## A Day In The Life Of A Fashion Designer

I, the fashion designer, make lovely clothes. I am inspired because of the style and poses. I focus on my designs, but I don't focus on anything else. Fashion's my life, that's what people say. It is true, it's my life for ever and ever. I make extremely fabulous designs. I think I can do better, people say they're fine. The ones with mirrors catch people's eyes and when I come to their town, they say 'Hey!' but they don't want to say goodbye. My favourite design is the one with flowers, those ones light the whole room and people are really amazed. The style of my designs is really cool. At the end of the stage there is a great, big pool. Around the pool there are my fascinating designs on pieces of paper for people to have a good look. One of my designs every factory likes. They give me an offer and take it. The designs that are really fashionable are the ones for spring and summer. When people come on stage, the music player is the drummer.

When I was nine, I was really interested in fashion design, from that day forward I wanted to be a fashion designer. The dress that is displayed outside the building is blooming with blue and green, wavy, blended-in colours. I will never lose my desire to be a fashion designer.

***Safoora Kamal (9)***
***Longfield Middle School***

## A Day In The Life Of A Spider

I have a total of eight legs and no wings, unlike human beings that have only two legs and no wings. Spiders can move very fast and they come in all sizes. Some spiders can be very furry. I, the spider, can be anywhere so that nobody can see me. I can hide in little cracks and under the floor.

The word 'spider' comes from an old English world that means 'spinner'.

Before the spider is born, it is in an egg and the eggs go in the sack. After a month it pops out of its egg and it can look after itself. There can be over a hundred eggs in the sack.

Spiders spin webs to catch insects. The spider spins webs that are very, very sticky, even though they are made out of silk and every time an insect like an ant, bee, wasp, fly or a butterfly gets stuck in the silk web, I eat it all up.

Some spiders are poisonous and these are the colours of the poisonous spiders: red, green, black or brown.

Spiders can be seen anywhere in the garden or in your house, but you can't see them because they can be hiding in the cracks.

***Daveena Patel (9)***
***Longfield Middle School***

## A Day In The Life Of An Aardvark

Hi, I'm Termy and I am an aardvark. So, you want to learn all about the one and only, yes that's right, aardvarks. Well, let me begin. I'm a baby aardvark. Well, grown-up aardvarks eat termites, but not me, certainly not! I have lovely warm milk from my mum's belly. I suck all the lovely warm milk. Sometimes, I suck so hard it hurts my mum's belly. I am six whole months old now and my mum promised me that I could go out with her tonight. I am so pleased, I can hardly wait. I will see my mum eat termites. They're insects you know, like ants.

Now you're most probably wondering where I live, well my mum and I live in a hole. Yes I know, very boring. All my home is a black, dark hole. Well, anyway, tonight I woke up at about nine o'clock (pm that is.) I set out with my mum and watched her with great interest all night long. Aardvarks sleep all day long and wake up at night and have food. Aardvarks are very good diggers. They dig tunnels out of the earth for their own homes.

***Sara Harman (9)***
***Longfield Middle School***

## A Day In The Life Of A Koala

Yum! Hi! My name is Koala. My favourite food is eucalyptus leaves. Koalas live in Australia. I live in a tree in Australia. This tree is a very special one because it has lots of eucalyptus leaves. Eucalyptus leaves are very special to us because that is the only thing we eat. Most of the other trees don't have as many eucalyptus leaves as mine. We're just like humans because we're mammals and we have ear flaps. Koalas sleep in the night and are awake in the day. We don't know who our ancestors are. Do you know, I've spent all day talking? I bet you think it's boring. Anyway, now it's night and I'm *not* going to bed. Wait a minute, I'm going to ask Mum I forgot to tell you I'm a baby Koala. Mum says I can go but she has to come too. Did I just see a human and a dog?
'Mum, let's get out of here. Mum, watch out!' I say.
Mum's unconscious, so I put my nose on my mother's tummy. I run out of there as fast as I can. There is danger in Australia, what with Black Widow spiders and scorpions, but the most dangerous thing to us koalas is man. Sometimes he kills us and eats us. Just like sharks eat man if they're in the sea. They come and gobble them up. It is unusual for a baby koala to carry its mother. It's supposed to be the other way round.
'What time is it?' I ask.
'Nap time,' Mum said. Goodbye.

***Jade Priest Hurley (9)***
***Longfield Middle School***

## A Day In The Life Of An Elephant

I am an elephant. My name is Ele, I live in a swamp. It is fun because I have friends that live there too. I am an African elephant. I have another species of elephants and they are called Asian elephants which live in Asia. I have ancestors, one of which is called a white elephant, and the other a woolly mammoth and they are very rare.

On hot summer days, I can toss dust through my trunk over my back to keep myself cool and clean. To keep cool, I use the same technique, but instead of dust, I use water. We also like play fighting and spray one another with water.

A baby elephant like me stays in its mother's tummy twice as long as a human baby. When Mummy is ready to give birth, the herd forms a protective circle around the mother-to-be. My aunt helps my mum to give birth to the baby. When the baby elephant is born, he learns quickly how to walk and he reaches out for food from small trees as he cannot reach the large trees. I can eat 50kg of food and water and my mum can eat up to 100kg of food and water.

When my grandad was killed, humans came and cut off his tusks and sold them for a lot of money. They sold his tusks as ornaments. We elephants can live up to a hundred years and this is my life story.

***Zarina Ilyas (9)***
***Longfield Middle School***

## A Day In The Life Of An Ant

I am an ant, I am a very small insect. I have six legs, which are very small. To me, a human is a colossal giant.

Some humans are very kind to ants because they do not kill us, but some humans are nasty and they kill us. When I see a human going to kill me, I try to run my fastest and hide. When I see a human trying to kill another ant, I feel very sad and I think that I should help, but I myself don't want to get killed. I have very little eyes so I can't see many things. Humans can kill us because they are many times faster than we ants.

When we are hungry, we can't find food on the ground so we try and eat cooked food from a human's plate, only sometimes we eat food from the ground.

We have to dig small holes in the ground and live in the holes. The Queen ant has the biggest hole. We dig the hole. We are born from the Queen ant, who is much bigger than we are. The Queen gives birth to lots and lots of baby ants per day. We ants have to build the baby ants' homes for them until they are old enough.

All ants hate to be in water. We definitely hate to be in deep water because we drown and then we sadly die.

***Amrit Mahbubani (9)***
***Longfield Middle School***

## A Day In The Life Of A Gorilla

Hello, I am Mr Joe. I'm the biggest gorilla in the world you know. I'm 27ft 4inches. Hey, could you be quiet for a minute, I can see a deer from behind those bushes and if you're quiet enough, I might be able to squash it to death so after, I can eat it.

I'm pretty lucky in a way for two things:
No.1 I'm so big that none of the animals in the wild try to attack me,
No.2 I live so far into the wild, no hunters try to hunt me down because they're too scared they won't find their way back.

Still there has been a time when there were fourteen, or was that fifteen hunters who tried to capture me. It was dreadful! I ran and ran but each minute they had me circled. Soon I rant out of land to escape into. I didn't like this, I didn't like it at all, but then again I became the lucky one. You see, when the hunters started firing their guns at me, a family of gorillas started helping me fight them back. These hunters were very skilful so they were quite a challenge for us. We struggled and struggled, but we wouldn't let that get in our way. We fought until the enemy had only one man left standing. We decided just to leave him, so he would run away for good. Oh look, the deer's got away. I'll have to go and get it!

***Gurpreet Tatla (9)***
***Longfield Middle School***

## GORILLAS

My name is Gorro; I live in a jungle not too far away from Mount Everest. I am 10 years old. My father is 41 years old and my mother is 37 years old. I am the only child in my family. My relatives also live with my parents and me. I always play with my cousins as I am an only child. We normally play 'had' or 'Simon says'. Sometimes my uncles, aunties and parents join in. People try to hunt me and my family, but we run deep into the jungle where hunters are scared because they cannot find their way back.

The gorillas are the unluckiest in the whole of the jungle. All the gorillas work as a team to find shelter and food for the other gorillas to survive in hot weather and have food to eat, such as rabbits and deer, so that they will not feel weak.

I have always tried to climb the whole of big Mount Everest, but it is way too high for me. Perhaps Mighty Joe (the biggest gorilla in the whole world) can climb it.

***Jaspal Singh Tatla (10)***
***Longfield Middle School***

## An Easter's Tale

'Mum, what are we having for dinner tonight?' said Baby Mouse.
'Mmm. Let me see. Oh dear, we seem to have nothing.' sighed Mother Mouse.
Father Mouse meanwhile, who was reading the Daily Mousehole was in shock.
'Don't worry,' said Baby Mouse, already trying to eat the furniture, 'we'll just poke our heads outside the hole and sniff out the food' and as soon as he could say 'blow me down' there on the dining room table, was the most delicious-looking Easter egg he had ever seen. 'Quick Mum, quick Dad, look what I see!' he shouted. Mother Mouse and Father Mouse ran over to him.
'What's the matter?' Father Mouse asked.
'Look up there!'
In astonishment, the whole of the mouse family looked up at the egg.
'Let's climb up and get it,' said Baby Mouse in excitement.
'I don't think that's very safe,' said Father Mouse, who was a bit of a coward.
But there was no stopping Baby Mouse. He had already started tying clothes together to make a rope. Finally, they all agreed that they should go up and get the Easter egg. Their first attempt was to climb up a rope (the one that Baby Mouse had made earlier with his clothes.) All the mice had a go at throwing the rope up onto the table, but all of their throws were feeble against the huge table. Their second attempt was just to climb up the chairs and jump onto the table, but for starters, none of them could climb up the leg of the first chair.

In the end, they were giving up hope until Baby Mouse had an idea. The house they lived in belonged to a family called the Williams family. They always left a mousetrap outside the door to the hole in the wall to catch the mice, but Baby Mouse was smarter than everyone thought. He thought that he could sit on the spring, Father Mouse to trigger it off and the spring would shoot Baby Mouse up to the top of the table.

Early next morning, Baby Mouse told his method of getting to the egg to Father Mouse and Mother Mouse. They all agreed that it was a good idea. So, Baby Mouse sat on the spring, Father Mouse triggered it and

my goodness, he shot up onto the table like a bullet from a gun.
'Mother, get my bed cover and you and Father hold it out to catch the egg' Baby Mouse shouted down to them.

Down below, Father and Mother Mouse were holding out Baby Mouse's bed cover. All of a sudden, Baby Mouse had pushed the egg and it tumbled down until it hit the bed cover, safely and softly. Then Baby Mouse jumped down himself and landed safely on the bed cover.

They all sat down straight away and started eating the egg. Then Baby Mouse said, 'This is the best dinner I've ever had!'

***Thomas Watson (11)***
***Longfield Middle School***

## THE DAY OF TUTANKHAMUN

I am Tutankhamun, many people don't know how I died. I died and then went in my tomb. It moaned and groaned because it had to keep robbers away from all the treasures of mine. It did a good job in fact my treasure was the only treasure that was not stolen. I told my tomb that I was going shopping but I wasn't, I was going to get my heart weighed? To go to the afterlife and if your heart is heavier than the feather of truth you don't go to the afterlife and get fed to one of the God's pet monsters. If it is the same or lighter you were allowed to go through to the afterlife and the monster would not have his lunch. So I go to get my heart weighed and yes! I am through to the afterlife.

***Grant Fynn (10)***
***Longfield Middle School***

## A Day In The Life Of A Butterfly

The day of a butterfly unfolds from its cocoon. Its pretty colours unfold. It flutters by its wings in full stretch. Purple, red, blue and white.

A butterfly must eat, sleep and keep its wings strong. As it flutters by the theme park and into the park past the trees that give us oxygen. Past the flowers where the bees do the job of spreading the pollen. The sun's shining. Until the rain comes back then it takes cover. The sun comes back out. So does the butterfly family. The butterfly is bored, so he has naps.

He wakes energetically and flies off, it will have to mate. It is hard to make female butterflies like you. First he shows off his colours but to no avail. He shows his flying speed but she still doesn't like him. A bee comes and he fights the bee off, they mate later on. He gets up in the morning tired. He now has a big day in front of him. He goes back to the theme park and half awake, almost got hit by a roller-coaster. He had a nap and saw a rainstorm and flew south.

***Michael Tredgett (10)***
***Longfield Middle School***

## A Day In The Life Of A Squirrel

Hello, my name is Nuts. I am a squirrel, I live in a hole and I eat lots and lots of nuts. Nuts are my favourite, I like them a lot, I eat lots in a day. I have nuts for breakfast, for lunch and for dinner. When I go to bed it makes me dream about them a lot. I eat nuts wherever I find them. I can even find them from peanut bags as whenever I smell peanuts I go to that place and find them. Then after I find them, I take as much as I can carry and take them back to my hole and then I start eating them.

It is really hard to find them, once you get to the place. They are sometimes all over the place. Once I have found them I have to run and run before they go into the bin. So I could find as many as possible and eat them up. I find them every day and then eat lots of them. One day I found a big bag of peanuts and once I found a big peanut. Before it went into the bin, I took it to my hole and ate it up. I only ate half. I ate half in the morning and half in the afternoon and half in the evening as well and it took hours!

***Pallavi Gajjar (9)***
***Longfield Middle School***

## A Day In The Life Of My Great, Great Grandfather's Son

I am inspired by my great, great grandfather's son because he had an interesting life. He was sailing to another country by boat and he was passing the World War II; his boat got hit but luckily he found a log in the sea and he held on to it and swam to shore.

He went to hospital to get checked and to see if he was OK. He was fine! I don't really know what happened after that, but after, whenever I went to his house he was really kind to me and my brother. Over on the other side of the bed he kept his books and whenever we came to my house when I was younger.

He used to be able to walk but when he got older he was disabled but he still came to my house and he still gave me sweets. He died when I was four. I was really sad but I still remember him mostly whenever I have sweets and mostly when my grandfather gives me sweets.

Whenever I see photos of him and me playing I always still think he's alive when he's actually dead. I think nearly everyone in my family still loves him and cares for him and still remembers him. I know I still do!

*Nina Parmar (9)*
*Longfield Middle School*

## A Day In The Life Of Me As An Adult

Dear Diary,
Today was the best day I ever had. It started off good because in the morning I spoke to my parents. They wanted to wish me a *Happy Birthday* as it was my birthday and *Good Luck* because I was starting my first proper job. I had got a job as a doctor in a hospital. I got to the hospital and I was given a tour. After that I went to the canteen for a coffee. When I came out of the canteen, there was a crowd of doctors and nurses. They were trying to save a patient who was in really bad condition. They didn't have enough people helping them so my instincts told me to help them.

Then a problem arose. Another patient came in and she was in the same condition as the other patient. The team split up and got to work. My team had to work quickly, our patient was losing blood. We put the patient into a stable position and then started operating. I sealed up the wound to stop the blood leaking. Our patient was slipping and for a second I thought that we were going to lose her. We finally finished operating. I had helped to save a person's life. I am so proud of myself. I had a party in the evening. It's been such a brilliant day and I will never forget it.

***Kaiya Chowdhary (12)***
***Priestmead Middle School***

## A DAY IN THE LIFE OF ALISON FACONTI (ME)

My day starts like any other . . . with Mum saying 'Don't forget this and do that!' I get up and get ready for school. I know I am a normal kid because I am not ready when my friends knock on the door for me. On the way to school is when I finish trying to wake up. In school I sit and listen to secrets to pass on.

When it is 9.00 we go in and that is when everyone walks so slowly they may as well be walking backwards. We sit through some lessons. Memty and I always pass insulting notes to Samlouis, whom I sit next to. At break time we storm downstairs and then do something that will get them noticed.

Then we go in for our break between breaks we call lessons. At lunchtime everyone scoffs their lunch and argues over who took two crisps when they were only offered one. The rest of the school day is the same. When I get home I retire to my chair. I eat dinner and go to the strange world of the park where it is never a normal day, always an adventure. I watch TV for ages then fall asleep at 3 - 5am. Goodnight!

***Alison Faconti (12)***
***Priestmead Middle School***

## A Day In The Life Of Me

Hello, my name is Katherine Louise Katy Franks and I have very gruesome, green skin. I also am 12,000,000,000 years old but I look like I am 120 years old but I am a lot older. I am very rich because I have 100,000,000,000,000,000,000 all in cash. Our coins are made out of emerald because we like green on my planet. My parents are a lot older than me because my mum is 41,000,000,000,000 and my dad is 49,000,000,000,000 and my brother is 9,000,000,000 and this is my home planet called Gloobe Slime. My friends are called Robo Cop who is very ill, Skunky and Timonha who are two babies and 1 adolescent.

***Katherine Franks (12)***
***Priestmead Middle School***

## A Day In The Life Of A Lost Polar Bear

It was dark and misty as the sun rose up in the sky, its rays reflecting on the beautiful, pure snow. At last the little polar bear awakes in search of his mother once again.

As he walks through the cold snow, trying to smell the footsteps of his mother. He wishes he had never wandered off, away from his mother. The polar bear only knows his name, (which is Iceberg), but otherwise nothing much. Iceberg walks to the lake as a funny looking creature approaches him; coming into the sunlight.

It is a human holding a very sharp spear in one arm and a plastic bag in the other. Iceberg hides his face with his medium-sized paws. Peeking through his paws he sees the hunter go. Iceberg turns the other way and runs trying not to be seen by the hunter.

Iceberg sees other little polar bears playing about near a cave. He joins them sneakily hoping they won't realise they have an extra cub. But their mother calls them in the cave one by one, counting and smelling them as they go in. So once again Iceberg runs away not wanting to cause trouble or disturbance.

As the sun sets down, Iceberg sets down to a lonely evening without his mum, but is sure to find her tomorrow as the sun rises.

***Rajenthini Varadarajah (12)***
***Priestmead Middle School***

## A Day In The Life Of My Friend Alison, The Dreaded Witch

A day in the life of Alison would be very cool in one way but very dangerous in another. Her day begins at around 7.00am where she appears from a puff of smoke in her deep, creepy and gloomy bedroom. The spiders retreat into the cracks in the walls they call home. She then has to go down to the kitchen, which they call the cauldron room, for they have a drink of slimy, gooey potion that makes them look more human than witch (long, crooked noses, big green warts etc). That made the witch not react to salt or not turn to stone at the sight of sunrise. She then has to get into her school uniform, which she loves because of the dull colours (grey, green and black). Nobody drops her to school in the mornings, they don't have to really because she bewitches herself so nobody can see her then flies on her cheap, ancient vacuum cleaner.

When she does finally get to school she puts her mode of transport behind the bike shed. She then walks through the school corridors and into her classes like everything's normal and nobody suspects a thing. The rest of the day is like any other except for when she wants to put someone into line who has stepped out (by magic of course). When she gets home she just sits on the sofa and doesn't move at all except for when she bewitches things to come to her like food, the remote control etc. Finally she vanishes at midnight with a puff of smoke!

***Samil Shah (12)***
***Priestmead Middle School***

## WORLD CUP WINNER

Dear Diary,
At 7.00am I woke up to go to see the England Manager, Alf Ramsay to get ready for the World Cup Final. We went on to Wembley's hallowed turf and then I started to talk to my fellow West Ham colleagues Geoff Hurst and Martin Peters.

Match time came very quickly and we were all raring to go but so were our opponents West Germany. We started very well and got a goal by Geoff Hurst. We broke through the German defence again and Martin Peters this time getting the goal.

The Germans were still determined to score and they were beating Banks. We were still 2-1 up, we were sure to win. It was the 90th minute but they got a free kick. Charlton closed the shot down but the ball slipped past him and Germany scored so it had to go to extra time. Both teams fought well but Geoff Hurst got through again and the ball hit the crossbar and came back down behind the goal line and the referee gave the goal to Hurst. We were 3-2 up, nothing could stop us.

We went on to score another goal by Hurst which gave him a hat-trick and England the joy of winning the World Cup. When I lifted the cup it was the most brilliant thing ever.

My story was about Bobby Moore who sadly died in 1992.

***Luke Peters (12)***
***Priestmead Middle School***

## A Day In The Life Of My Mother

Dear Diary,

Monday: Had a boring day, very busy.

Tuesday: Did all my homework, extremely exhausted.

Wednesday: Fab, great time at the disco.

Thursday: Came from school. Realised that my mum is always busy. Doing this, or that. Kept an eye on her to see what she was up to, washing the dishes, ironing the clothes, cooking for dinner and much, much more. Sometimes I say . . . imagine if I was her? Once, only once I would be my own mother and I would do everything she does . . . what do you think? Well I'll have a go.

Friday: Woke up at 7.00am *trying* to make breakfast. Everybody woke up at 8.00am and were growling about the time whereas I was relaxing and waiting for my watch to 'beep' for 8.30am. When my watch struck 8.30am I left a note saying 'I'll come from school at 12.05 to make lunch and don't make dinner'. At 12.10 I made toasted sandwiches. How hard could that be? In the evening it took me one hour and 45 minutes to make dinner. We were having noodles! They were microwave noodles as well! It's really because my microwave had problems so I took 45 minutes on that. 15 minutes later I got totally annoyed and boiled them. Oops! It didn't turn out quite well so we just ordered Domino's pizzas.

***Shweta Dattani (11)***
***Priestmead Middle School***

## A Day In The Life Of Mrs Carter-Coombes (Teacher)

Mrs Carter-Coombes is quite an ugly woman. She has got a really skinny body and spots and freckles all over her face. She has even got a moustache! Her dress sense is absolutely outrageous. She wears flowery, fluorescent clothes and she wears trainers under her clothes.

She gets up in the morning forgetting that she has homework to mark. She finishes all her marking in 20 minutes (the marking is always wrong). After marking she has breakfast and leaves to go to school. She usually meets Mr Wilson who is as ugly as her - he wears teletubbies ties to work (he's a lawyer).

Mrs Carter usually tells him 'Why hello Mr Wilson and how are you this fine and sunny morning?' Mr Wilson replies 'Very fine thank you, why you look more beautiful by the day' trying to fake an accent.

When Mrs Carter gets to school (she is always late) she blames the traffic for being late. She teaches Year 9 (who are really naughty) she spends the whole day telling Peter Walker off who is always making fun of her. Mrs Carter-Coombes totally freaks out! She does not even get along with the teachers, even they say she is really weird.

That's Mrs Carter-Coombes' day at work. When she gets home she has dinner. Gets into her pink and orange fluorescent pyjamas and goes to sleep.

***Samina Omar (12)***
***Priestmead Middle School***

## A Day In The Life Of Michael Owen

I woke up suddenly after having a nightmare about what I'm going to do about keeping Louise cheerful and then yesterday night she goes on about me not spending enough time with her. While in bed I was thinking where I could take her out, or shall I invite her to a romantic dinner at home and suddenly I realised that I was running late for my training session.

So I jumped out of bed and had a quick, hot shower and skipped breakfast and ran to the car. Then unluckily on my way to the training session I got the fifth speeding ticket in two weeks. As I was changing I was beginning to think 'Oh no' not another six hours of training in this drizzling rain.

Today was one of my worst training sessions because Gerard Houllier was angry at me considering I was not passing the ball properly to my colleagues. After three hours of hard training we had a nice, relaxing one hour lunch break. After lunch we had another three hours of training.

As soon as I got home I rang Louise and invited her to a romantic dinner but Louise declined the invitation as she was not feeling well. So in the end I ended up with a take-away pizza and a bottle of wine and video to watch. At eleven o'clock I went to bed and I thought 'It wasn't my day'.

***Kushal Shah (12)***
***Priestmead Middle School***

## A Day In The Life Of Mick Foley

I woke up feeling nervous today. I had a WWF title shot. But it was against The Rock. I walked into the Raw is War stadium later that day and walked into the cafeteria and sat down. Everyone was giving me good luck although we knew who would win.

A couple of hours later I was getting ready to go out to the ring. I can still hear the words going on in my head 'If ya smell what The Rock is cooking.' After D Generation X were at the side of the ring and so were The Corporation. We started the match circling round the ring and then *bang!* we started fighting. There were punches, kicks and wrestling moves. By this time D Generation X and The Corporation were battling and the referee went out to stop them. None of them heard the breaking of glass from Stone Cold's music. Now Stone Cold had been out for 2 months so everyone was excited. He came running in with a steel chair and *wham!* hits The Rock and I cover him and the referee counts 1-2-3. I become the new WWF Champion. D Generation X started to parade me round the ring and out.

***Todd Davies (12)***
***Priestmead Middle School***

## A DAY IN THE LIFE OF A FOX

Sally was at school on the day before half-term started and it was play time. She was playing hide-and-seek and her friend Jane was it. Jane had found Sally first and was trying to find everyone else when Sally accidentally blurted out that she was going to the forest for a trip. She wasn't supposed to say anything but she was trying to make Jane jealous. She told Jane to keep it a secret.

When the day finally came, they all got ready to leave at about 9.00am. When they reached the forest in half an hour, they saw a fox in front of them. Sally's sister put her hand out to stroke it. It nearly bit her, but Sally managed to pull her sister's hand out of the way. They followed the fox to where it fed himself. They said it was weird because they saw it eat twigs and nuts. Its food was strange and sometimes it stopped eating, went to excrete and then started to eat again. When it began to eat anything it saw, we thought it had turned bonkers, but then realised that its mother probably left him at birth and that's why it probably didn't know how and which foods to eat.

The fox then went to sleep and its bed looked warm. It slept peacefully with little noises now and again and looking at it made everyone go to sleep. When it woke up the next morning, Sally and her family woke up too because it made a strange stretching sound. It went to look for breakfast and when the sleepy family saw a mouse by the tree they knew that there was going to be trouble. The fox saw the mouse and started chasing it. The mouse got caught and sadly eaten. The fox took the mouse's bare bones into its hole and as Sally and her family wouldn't be able to fit in the hole, her adventure was to come to an end.

Sally thought it was magnificent to see the life of a fox. When she got back to school after her holidays, she told everyone about her day. She had had a brilliant time.

***Nilma Shah (12)***
***Priestmead Middle School***

## A Day In The Life Of Me

Dear Diary
It's me Azaleara Watercress. Just got back from the park. Went there with Rubber Woolworths and met up with Hula Hoops original, Ant-Sat-On-A-Knee, Road Toad and Baz Adventure. We went to a Happy Shopper and got some food. We have made a new song up, as our last four reached number one. I'll tell you a bit of it.

There's a fox
in the house
and nobody knows

Do you like it?
I'll get back to you tomorrow.

Sorry, I didn't get back to you sooner, I've been recording and making the video to our new song. Next week we are going to Top Of The Pops. In 7 months we're going on tour around America. The fans just love us there. We have got three concerts at Wembley next year and three in Manchester a week later. Now we have become more popular we are so busy. Plus we have to keep up with our school work. Anyway what's happening in your life?

Oh, oh before I forget, our album is coming out in September it will be called 'Where's the fox'?

PS - Don't forget to buy our album next month.

***Aaron Gilchrist (12)***
***Priestmead Middle School***

## A Day In The Life Of A Headteacher

It all started one day at a school called Old Elm which was in Boggling. It had a strange girl called Geri who wanted to know what it was like being a headteacher. Her friend Jane wanted to know why Geri was acting strange. So Geri told Jane that she was going to follow the stupid headteacher. Jane didn't agree with her and started to fight. But they were friends.

So one day, she went to the office where the headteacher worked. She slowly opened the door and searched around to see if there was anything which was very important. Geri found every child's file and a computer. There was a tall bottle of pickles which Geri found disgusting. Suddenly, there was a big bang and Geri heard footsteps coming towards the room. Her heart was beating faster and Geri went to hide under the table. There was a visitor with the headteacher when he entered into the room. They were talking.

After the visitor went the headteacher prepared what he was going to say in Assembly. Geri found out it was hard being a headteacher because you have to sort budgets and other big things. She learnt this in the week. The headteacher was putting something in the bin and Geri was spotted under the table. She was in big trouble and when I mean trouble she had to clean toilets for a week. After this she knew never to follow the headteacher again. This story has no end, this story has no moral but now it has finished.

***Rowena Shah (12)***
***Priestmead Middle School***

## A Day In The Life Of A Teacher

There is a year 7 teacher at Bromley Middle School. She is a horrible teacher. The teacher's name is Miss Slangly. Her day is pretty boring. It starts off with her having a cigarette. During school she is really horrible. All she does is shout. She smells of coffee and smoke. Believe me she smells. A girl called Louis, she was a new girl in school, she followed Miss Slangly. She wanted to know what that teacher's life was like. She went downstairs in the room. She had a smoke. It smelled really bad, it was getting to her throat and she was coughing. She knew that I was following her.
She said 'Do you want something?'
Louis said 'Yes, why are you horrible to the pupils?'
She said 'I just teach you all and I get my money from the headmaster.'
I said 'Do you like people?'
'No, I don't hate people.'
'Can't you be a bit nice or a lot nicer to people? Can you try just for me?'
Miss Slangly was very upset, she had never been upset before.
She said 'I could be a bit nicer.'
So they both came upstairs. Louis's friends said 'What happened?'
She said 'I just talked to her.'
'What did you say?'
'You will find out.'

When people were in her class for lessons she does a lot of shouting but when I came in she was kind and not horrible to us. Everyone liked this teacher, now she was funny.

***Menisha Chauhan (11)***
***Priestmead Middle School***

## Postman Sam Delivers Again

Characters: Postman Sam, Mrs Dumpling, Mr 'O' Dodo, Mr Rondongong, Mrs Dingbat, Mr and Mrs Adlingstoneys, Mrs Lobstergobster.
Setting: Town of Harstone.

A day in the life of Postman Samson is him having to get up really early, having breakfast all by 6.30. He has to be at the sorting office by 7.00. While he is delivering a big, heavy bag of mail he sees Mrs Dumpling walking her dog like he does every day at 7.10. After a few roads he gets to the shops and buys a drink.

He then carries on with his post bag. As he walks past the park he sees Mr O'Dodo with Mr Rondongong walking their dogs. As he approached Mrs Dingbat's house (a widow) she had a lot of different cards with coloured envelopes so he thought it was her birthday.

A street down as he came to the first couple of houses there were postcards going to the neighbours of Mr and Mrs Adlingstoneys who are in Ameraustwalefranltalscotirelanengish. He had fun reading the postcards. After he had delivered the rest of the mail down that road he had nothing left so he had to go back to the sorting office. He found that there was no mail so he went home and relaxed.

***Tomos Jones (12)***
***Priestmead Middle School***

## A Day In The Life Of A Professional Snooker Player

I will guide you on what I think it feels like in the day of a professional snooker player. If I were playing I would be tense because the other players might beat me. If the other players are good, you have to work extra hard. To impress them you might use your personal skills or tactics. I think you will find it very interesting. When you are playing a shot, try to keep calm and cool.

Snooker is a sport and two to four people can play it. The bad thing is when you are losing and getting up early to practise. The good thing is when you are playing against them and it is challenging for you to play with. If you re in the finals in the Crucible and it is your first time there, you will be really tense because the audience will be watching you.

If you have won the competition you will get a big cup and you might feel shy because you might not have won anything in your life. So how did it feel?

We hope you had a great time here!

***Kishan Sitapara (12)***
***Priestmead Middle School***

## A Day In The Life Of A Prime Minister

7.30am - I say goodbye to my wife, who is getting ready for work and kids who are getting prepared for school. There wasn't time for breakfast.

7.35am - I meet my chauffeur James and the Chancellor of the Exchequer. I instruct him to drive us to the Houses of Parliament.

8.00am - We arrive at the Houses of Parliament, and separate by going to our offices. When I reach my office my secretary tells me shocking news. There has been a bomb on Victoria Station. An estimate of thirty people have been killed.

9.00am - I make a televised speech to the media that I am saddened and appalled at these senseless murders of these innocent people and I will do everything in my power to find the bombers.

11.00am - I have to answer questions in Prime Minister's Question Time. I struggled to answer some of the questions, as I would've liked to do.

12.00pm - I have lunch at the Houses of Parliament, while I eat I meet the Foreign Minister who tells me the Queen's visit to Australia was a success.

2.00pm - My secretary and me set off in my limousine and tell James to drive us to the NEC arena in Birmingham for the Children of Courage Award ceremony.

4.15pm - We arrive at the NEC arena and give awards to all the brave children who have been honoured and sign autographs.

5.00pm - We leave the arena and go home.

7.45pm - I reach home, eat dinner, have a bath, put the children to sleep and sleep myself.

***Krishen Shah (12)***
***Priestmead Middle School***

## A Day In The Life Of Libby Stocker

Amy, my best friend and I were walking to school together. Amy wasn't acting herself, it was as if she was Libby Stocker. She walked like a model and acted like a real bully, this was only because she was one. When we reached school, Libby came up to me! She was really nice, we talked about boys and music. I have never had a chat like that with anyone but I thought it was really fun.

When Amy saw me chatting to Libby she got really mad so she started to hit me and punch me. After she had finished I flooded with tears. Libby came up to me, exactly the same way Amy would and asked me what was wrong? Then only did I realise that they were both switched around.

To me this didn't make any sense because Libby went up to Amy and started to do the same things that Amy did to me. Mr Flitcharm, our Science teacher, saw them and called Libby in. Amy and I didn't know who was who. Then we started to talk and I knew that this was the real Amy. When we were about to go inside, Libby the real one said that she is on a warning of being suspended. We were shocked!

Libby, of course, was very worried about this so on our last break we all played together. Mr Flitcharm was pleased to see that!

***Heeral Shah (12)***
***Priestmead Middle School***

## A Day In The Life Of Jamina

Grandfather and I are following a honey bird. We come to a really, lovely lake. I spoke to Grandfather and said 'I would really like to see a real elephant.'
'You won't see many these days, since the hunters came' said Grandfather.
'Oh I do want to be a hunter.'
I am playing hunters, agh now I am lost. I wandered too far into the bush. As a tear trickled down my cheek, I'm scared.

I heard another cry just like mine. I went to see what it was. It's a baby elephant, his mum was dead. I whispered 'I will never be a hunter.' I patted him. After a while he trusted me. We walked along the dust path. We saw some zebras, we still walked on and on.

Then we saw hungry crocodiles in a lake. I said 'Let's go on.' Then elephants are around me. They take this elephant and he said 'My mum has come to take me home.'

***Thomas Owen (9)***
***St Lawrence RC School, Feltham***

## A Day In The Life Of A Baby Elephant

'Oh no, my mum would not wake up, the sun is really hot. I cannot stand the heat and there is no water for miles, how will I survive?'

Now I will try and go to the river. Then I see a girl and I looked at the water and I see my reflection and that I am an elephant. I have a big, long trunk, two big ears, four big feet and a little tail and I am grey all over. I look in the water again and I see a crocodile. He looks like he's hungry and I think he wants us to lunch.

We run as fast as we can, he is really, really slow so he goes back into the water. I ask the little girl 'What is your name?'
She replies 'My name is Jamina.'

Me and Jamina see some poachers killing an elephant then we run away. Me and Jamina see some elephants then go with them and I say 'Goodbye' before I go.

***Linno Soares (9)***
***St Lawrence RC School, Feltham***

## A Day In The Life Of A Crocodile

I have just got back from the long trip down the river. I'm so tired. It is so hot that all the reeds are dead. I see someone's shadow. Wait, I see two. Should I eat them? No, I don't think so. I should see if they are good. 'How are you?'
'Fine, thank you.' I knew that she sensed danger because she did not cross this way.

I see some zebras coming to have a drink. I wanted some dinner. I dived down into the water as one of the zebras approached to have a drink. I pounce on one and pulled them into the water. I made it drown, then I ate the zebra for dinner.

I swam to the other side of the river to my surprise I saw some poachers looking for elephants. They spotted some on the other side of the river. He went to cross the river. I took a bite out of his leg. He fell to the ground. He was dead. I just saved some elephants from death.

I went to sleep. The next morning I went back down to the river.

***Joshua Ssali (9)***
***St Lawrence RC School, Feltham***

## A Day In The Life Of A Baby Elephant

I'm all alone in the jungle. My mum is asleep. Why won't she get up? Now I'm really hot, the sun is scorching down on me. All of a sudden I hear rustling in the bushes!

Now I wander on and on I see sanctuary and water 'hooray'. But I speak too soon, poachers surround me. 'Hello elephant' they say in a dark, cruel voice. But I show them, I get them by my trunk and throw them in the water.

Then a dear child comes and takes me away. We walk up the high, steep mountains with crowing vultures above us. We sneakily jump on the crocodiles but the last one took us under. Somehow we survived. We trundled home all wet and soggy. Then a herd of elephants were standing in front of us. I had to go with them. I waved goodbye to Jamina then off I went.

***Joseph Everett (9)***
***St Lawrence RC School, Feltham***

## A DAY IN THE LIFE OF A ZEBRA

One day I was walking through the plains in Africa. It was boiling hot so I decided to head for the river.

When I got there I started to drink straight away because I was really thirsty. A log appeared from nowhere and it was floating towards me. I realised it had eyes, it must be a crocodile. I ran as fast as my feet would allow.

I got to the jungle. I was very hungry. A herd of elephants came racing by. After they had gone lots of fruit had fallen to the ground. Oranges, apples, bananas and grapefruits were everywhere. I started to eat but soon I could hear the herd of zebras. I ran to the plains - there they were, hooray!

***Jack Devereux (9)***
***St Lawrence RC School, Feltham***

## A Day In The Life Of A Baby Elephant

Me and my mum came to Africa in this flying machine. Somehow I was all alone with my mum, then other animals, like zebras, crocodiles and elephants came.

Then poachers came and killed my mum. A girl came along and she stroked me on the back, but I was all sad.

She told me her name, she was called Jeammla, it was the same as my mum's name. She told me she was not a poacher so I walked with her for hours. Then we saw some poachers so we hid.

When they went past us we carried on walking. Then we fell asleep and I had a dream of elephants taking me back. When I woke up the elephants were there so I went with them.

***Aaron O'Sullivan (9)***
***St Lawrence RC School, Feltham***

## A DAY IN THE LIFE OF JAMINA

Grandad has just asked me to go for a walk in the jungle. I am excited because I might see hunters, wild animals and poachers. Grandad and I set off. It was a really hot, boiling day and I was tired. The sun got even hotter. I ask Grandad if I can play hunters. I turn my head around and turn back to see if Grandad was there, but he wasn't. My tears come running down my little face.

When I started to walk I suddenly heard someone crying in the direction I was going. It was coming from behind the bushes. Grandad always advises me not to approach the bushes if there is a sound, without an adult. I notice that it is a baby elephant. It was trying to wake its mother but she has been killed by hunters. The baby elephant didn't know that his mother was killed by the hunters. The baby elephant was trying to reach for some bananas but his trunk was too short and he is too tired to do anything. So I picked it up for the baby elephant.

I take him with me to look for elephants. It took us a long time till we came to a lake where there were crocodiles. Grandad says 'If you are lost always go to the lake and home is across it.' We entered the lake and a crocodile came to us and said 'I am going to eat you' and his mouth opened wide . . .

***Natalina Fashoda (9)***
***St Lawrence RC School, Feltham***

## A Day In The Life Of A Baby Elephant

Deep in the African jungle it is scorching hot and I am lonely and unhappy. I keep trying to wake my mum up but she won't wake up. I can hardly imagine that a few minutes ago she was getting me a banana and then fell down with a thud.

I am hungry and thirsty I try to reach the fruit tree with my trunk but I am getting more tired every minute. Finally I get some fruit but then I hear rustlings, could it be poachers? I run to the river and have a drink of water, then I go to see if my mum is awake.

When I see my mum is not moving, I realise she is dead. I am very sad. Then I hear more rustlings. I look around and see a little girl. I walk over to her and she comforts me. Then she tells me to come with her and I do. We walk and walk and walk, until I get tired but I had to go a little further, so I did. We saw the zebras and followed them to the river.

It is raining now and I am getting cold but we can't cross the river, it is too dangerous. We lie down under the palm trees and fall asleep. As we sleep the sun shines. I dream that I have my mother and when I wake up I see herds of elephants and the little girl tells me to go with them. As I turn around to say goodbye to the little girl, I see the sunset as a pinky-orangey colour, then I turn to go with the elephants.

***Kathryn Mellon (9)***
***St Lawrence RC School, Feltham***

## A Day In The Life Of A Baby Elephant

Deep inside the dark jungle there my mother is lying on the dusty floor. I call my mother's name but in my amazement she doesn't wake up. I feel sad and lonely, like nobody is there for me.

Then I start crying for help loud enough so that somebody could hear me. But in my astonishment a kind and loving person hears me and comes over. She says 'Are you OK?' I tried to answer her but I couldn't.

So I just lifted my trunk into her hand and we became friends. While we were walking I was saying in my mind that she was a nice, loving girl and that she loved animals, especially elephants. Then we arrived at the lake and she said to me 'We have to get across, but how?' Then we walk. We sit down for a rest but we fall asleep. When we wake up we finally find my family.

***Florence Proctor (9)***
***St Lawrence RC School, Feltham***

## A Day In The Life Of A Crocodile

It is a good morning and the sun is in the sky. Jamina and her grandfather followed the honey bird. Jamina heard a noise, it was the noise of a crocodile. I, the crocodile, have cornered my prey. I lift and *snap* on the zebra's leg.

Jamina goes home with her grandfather but she has to watch the crocodile.

***Debora Lopes (9)***
***St Lawrence RC School, Feltham***

## A Day In The Life Of A Baby Elephant

I feel sad and lonely because my mum won't wake up. The poachers came but I don't know what they did. It was raining, humid, dusty too. I am so hungry. I will go to the tree and get some bananas. I went back for my mum. I scratched her but she didn't wake up.

I'm thirsty so I might go to the river to get a drink with my long trunk. I can see my reflection. I looked in the water and I can see a crocodile waiting for its prey. I see lots of animals, like birds, honey birds and normal birds.

I am still worried and worn out from walking. The hunter might come and do what they did to my mum. I don't know what to do.

***Jamie Barlow (9)***
***St Lawrence RC School, Feltham***

## A Day In The Life Of A Baby Elephant

The heat in Africa today is scorching and I'm trying to wake my mum up. I shake her but she still won't wake up. I feel very sad, alone and frightened.

I'm very thirsty because elephants like water but there is no water to be seen in sight. It is getting so hot I cannot bare it anymore. But then a lost and kind girl comes over to me strokes me.

Then suddenly I hear voices behind the bushes, now I feel very scared. The little girl and I decide to hide behind another bush until they disappear. We go on a journey and meet the crocodile by the river and I also meet some zebras.

The little girl and I fall asleep and wake up to a herd of elephants, then we hear poachers again which scares the herd of elephants away. But we just stand there listening, wondering what to do next.

***Rachel Welch (9)***
***St Lawrence RC School, Feltham***

## A Day In The Life Of Jamina, An African Girl

It is a hot, humid, dusty day in Africa, me and my grandad go for a walk. I am excited, I might see a hunter. But then I pretend to be a hunter. I turn my small head to look for my grandad and a tear runs all the way down my cheek, my grandad had gone, I've walked too far. I hear a cry near enough like mine. I had to take the chance to see who it is.

It is a poor baby elephant scratching its mum. I slowly wipe my wet, tired face dry and comfort the poor, worried, sad elephant. Because its mum has been killed by a bad hunter. I had decided to bring the baby elephant with me. I feel as safe as houses.

We start our journey. The baby elephant stops and tries to go back. I look around carefully so nobody can see me. *It's a hunter!* We see him but he doesn't see us. The elephant is so scared he nearly falls head over heels into the river.

It's getting late, the elephant can't go any further, so I let him and me fall asleep. I would love to have a wonderful dream about my mum and grandad but I cannot. The only thing I can dream about is elephants. That's funny because when I woke up from my funny sleep, elephants were all around me. I wasn't scared at all. I let the baby elephant go and I said a sad goodbye and they went off and I fell asleep again. In the morning my mum found me and, I tell you, I was tired. I stayed close to my mum and remembered my journey every single step!

***Rachel Haldane (8)***
***St Lawrence RC School, Feltham***

## A DAY IN THE LIFE OF JAMINA

My name is Jamina, I live in Africa with my grandfather and my mum.

Today my grandfather said to me 'I am going to take you to the jungle.' I was so excited. We finally reached the jungle. Inside the jungle there were some strange plants and loads of shady places. All of a sudden I thought I heard poachers, then I pretended to be a *hunter!* When I turned my little head, I realised that I had gone too far into the jungle and there was no sign of Grandfather. I walked along feeling sad and lonely.

After a while I heard the cry of a baby elephant. I went to investigate. There I saw a baby elephant weeping because his mother had been killed by poachers. First of all the elephant was very scared, then I said in a soft voice 'I am not a hunter, come with me, we will try and find more elephants to look after you.'

Suddenly I remembered what Grandfather had told me. 'Follow the midnight herds, then you will come to a river, home is on the other side.' It's taking us ages to find the midnight herds. We have now found them. We are walking towards the river, we are there. Just a minute ago a honey bird said to us 'You can't cross this river, carry on, on your journey.' We are too tired to carry on. We have found some grass, we will sleep here tonight.

It is now morning. Standing in front of me are elephants. I have given them the little one. In the far distance I can see Mum. Mum is running towards me and I am running towards her. Now we are heading for home, I am staying very close to Mum all the way home.

***Christie Braham (9)***
***St Lawrence RC School, Feltham***

## A Day In The Life Of A Baby Elephant

Oh no, I think my mum has got killed by the hunters in this boiling, hot jungle in Africa. I feel so lonely. Then I see a small girl coming and I feel a little better because she is talking to me. I don't feel upset or lonely because I know she will look after me. I look at my reflection in the water and I see I'm a boring elephant like my mum.

This little girl takes me on a journey but I still don't know her name. On our journey we see in the sunset, zebras. The little girl told me that her name is Jamina. Jamina goes to sleep, leaving me in the boiling, humid weather. She wished her mum would call but instead, a herd of elephants came.

Jamina and me went back to the place where the hunter had been. I saw my mum, the elephant, calling. I was delighted to see her waking up. Then Jamina's mum was calling her, she was so happy.

***Jessica Browne (9)***
***St Lawrence RC School, Feltham***

## A DAY IN THE LIFE OF A BABY ELEPHANT

My mum is sleeping on her side. I'm waving my trunk enthusiastically trying to wake. There was rustling in the bushes, what could it be?

A girl came out of the bush and started to pat me, she cared about me. We went walking in the scorching heat, as we stumbled on in search of the herd.

*Bang!* I heard a poacher's gun and got worried, they were in sight. We majestically sneaked past them without them noticing.

I couldn't go on until I had water, then it started to rain. We had a drink and carried on through the storm.

When we thought we were lost forever, we fell asleep. We woke to the sound of elephants' feet. I turned around and saw my herd. The girl went away and we also went away to find shelter for the night. By the time we finally found shelter it was really dark and shadows were moving in the moonlight. Suddenly a group of armed poachers came out of the mist and started to catch us. I tried to escape but they were just too quick for me. They took me away and used me to carry logs and take people to places. Man! Will I ever escape from this poacher's paradise?

***Luke Taylor (9)***
***St Lawrence RC School, Feltham***

## A Day In The Life Of A Crocodile

Today I feel *sooo* hungry! I need food and I need it now! I can't relax in the hot water of this small billabong. I'm too hot out in the sun and now the water is drying up so I have to get out onto the dusty, hot sand. I just don't see why most crocodiles have to live in places as hot as Africa. If it carries on I'll die!

*Oh, oh*, I hear poachers coming and if they come near me I'll bite 'em!

I can hear some more poachers now but I'm not one little bit scared. Now I know that voice, but who is the other one? I can now see that it is a small African girl and a baby elephant. I can hear her saying, 'Come on, it's not safe to cross here,' and she walks away. But I now see the poachers and I would like to know what they are doing!

Just now I saw some poachers. Here they are again, but this time a man in a grey hat is coming over with a knife and now he's putting his hand in the water. If he puts his hand in my mouth I am going to . . . *snap!*

***Francesca Barry (9)***
***St Lawrence RC School, Feltham***

## A Day In The Life Of A Baby Elephant

I am hot, thirsty and hungry. I feel lonely and unsafe because my mum won't wake up. I'm saying to her 'I'm only a baby elephant.' All I want to do is wake my mum up. *'Please Mum get up!'* I'm shouting that out in hope she will open her eyes. 'Get up and fetch some of that delicious fruit, high up in the tree.'

I cried and cried. Luckily someone heard me. She talked to me, she said 'I'm lost, I am trying to find my way home. Would you like to come with me on my journey?'

Me and Jamina started our long journey through the hot African sun. Halfway through our journey we met some zebras. We followed the zebras till we got to the river. Jamina said to me she sensed danger there. So we walked away from the river. It started to rain. The rain got heavier and heavier and I got even more tired. Me and Jamina froze because we heard a noise. When the noise went away, me and Jamina walked on.

I finally got to the stage where I couldn't walk any longer. Me and Jamina sat down. She laid on me and we both went to sleep. When we woke up there were elephants all around us. I heard Jamina say before she gave me to them 'Look after this little one.'

***Amber-Rose Cox (9)***
***St Lawrence RC School, Feltham***

## A Day In The Life Of A Baby Elephant

I was in the long grass trying to reach a banana from a banana tree. But I was too small. My mum was lying helplessly on the ground. My tummy was rumbling hungrily. I decided to go to the river to have a drink. But there were scary, deadly eyes watching me.

I also saw figures standing in the background, hiding behind trees. The figures were holding guns! I sensed danger and trotted into the jungle. I heard strange noises in the jungle. I was frightened. I decided to look for some more food and water.

I finally found a banana on the ground below a banana tree. There was a big rock with some rainwater on it. I licked it up quickly and galloped further into the jungle.

I then fell asleep and when I woke up, lots of elephants were surrounding me! I got up and told them that my mum had died. Then I asked them if I could stay with them. They said 'Yes.' They had one other baby. I played with him. I lived happily ever after.

***Estelle Johnson (9)***
***St Lawrence RC School, Feltham***

## A Day In The Life Of My Dad

It's six o'clock in the morning, on Sunday 4th June 2000 and it is time for me to get up. I am trying to be as quiet as possible, not to wake the whole family. After I have had a shower, I come downstairs and have a quick cup of tea. It's now six-thirty and time to go to work. The roads are very quiet and I am at work by six-forty five. At my office I look on the computer to check what flights are about to land. I check to make sure that my radio is working and that I have all my passes to let me get into all the parts of the airport that only people with the correct passes can go.

When I arrive at the plane, there are lots of people around and it's my job to search the plane for drugs, along with other officers. We have a special dog to help us search the planes. It's three o'clock and it's the end of my shift, I can now go home.

It's three-thirty in the afternoon and now I can relax. My son and I watch the football on TV. After the football is finished we all sit down to dinner. At about eleven thirty I am ready to go to bed.
Goodnight, *Zzzzzzzzzzzzzzz!*

***Mark Davies (11)***
***Saxon Primary School***

## A DAY IN THE LIFE OF DENNIS WISE

First of all I get changed. Then I have my breakfast and have a very short training lesson. We start to talk about all of the team tactics, formation and the starting line up. I get changed into my suit, then we go onto the coach. We arrive at Wembley and get off onto the pitch, the reaction is spectacular. The crowd is roaring and interviewers come up to me and ask me how I feel about the FA Cup Final. I felt really confident.

We all go into the changing rooms and get changed into our football kit. We go over the team tactics one more time then we line up. When we got onto the pitch it was amazing, too good to explain. The whistle went, the match had started. Aston Villa had made a great start, they were really controlling possession. The half-time whistle was just blown Aston Villa were unfortunate not to have scored a goal. Vialli had a good word with us. It had got some sense into us. We came back onto the pitch feeling really confident. We kicked off, we started taking possession of the ball. I was making some brilliant opportunities. Roberto Di Matteo made a lovely ball through the middle, I struck it.

The next thing I knew was the whole Chelsea supporters cheering, but the referee told me I was off-side, I couldn't believe it. I got tripped just outside the penalty area, it was a free kick. Zola took it. It was swerving. Their goalkeeper came out he couldn't get to it. Roberto Di Matteo shot, it was a goal. Finally the whistle went. Chelsea were the new FA Cup champions. The Chelsea roar was explosive. I went up first, as I am the captain, I took my four month old boy, Henry, up as well and I lifted yet again the FA Cup. We opened champagne to celebrate our victory and we went back to Stamford Bridge with the FA Cup.

***Greg Stabler (11)***
***Saxon Primary School***

## A DAY IN THE LIFE OF A FROG

I woke up on my lily pad and jumped in the pond. After I had my early morning dip, I had some breakfast. I had three green flies. After I had my breakfast I went exploring round the garden. And when I was exploring I bumped into a horrible cat. It tried to scratch me, so I jumped on his nose. Then he tried to do it again but I jumped out of the way and it scratched itself on the nose and I hopped off.

A couple of hours later I was beginning to get dried out. So I began to hop back to my pond and two children caught me and put me in a bucket and left me in there for ages. A few hours later they put a really big frog in with me. When they went in to have their dinner, they didn't put anything over the top to stop the big frog from jumping out. Me and the big frog jumped in the pond and the big frog swam away. I jumped on my lily pad and had a rest and my tea. What a day I had.

***Charlie Cusack (11)***
***Saxon Primary School***

## A Day In The Life Of A Stag Beetle

It was a sunny day and my black skin was so hot it was going light brown. I was in my house, not big at all. When I decided I would have a stroll around the jungle. On my way I noticed that no bugs were out sunbathing and taking a walk or anything. Strangely thinking hard I walked along feeling hot and bothered. I thought about the hot sun and people all in their houses. As I walked, all of a sudden a dark shadow, the shape of a human's foot came down. *Splat!* I opened my eyes and luckily I was stuck in this horrible sticky stuff that humans chew in their mouths. The human female or male saw me and said '*Oow* a bug!' and flicked me off. I went flying in the air and landed in a huge tree, really wide and bushy.

When I opened my eyes I was still stuck in that horrible sticky stuff. No wonder bugs weren't out, they must have hid in their houses. My friend came up and helped me get out of the sticky stuff. When I got out I said 'Thanks,' then I shot across the jungle and got in my house. I phoned my friend and said 'Thank you,' then I got out my match box suitcase and started packing, like all the other bugs.

The humans were trampling all over towns. I packed everything and went over to my friend's house.
'Are you ready?' I said.
My friend said 'Yes.' And that's when we made our escape. Later on we went back to see our town and saw all the houses were crumbled up on the floor. All the bugs came back and started rebuilding their houses. When it was all done we went in and unpacked. So if it wasn't for my pal bug, I would still be in the bush with that horrible sticky stuff on me.

***Alicia Irwin (11)***
***Saxon Primary School***

## A Day In The Life Of A Paramedic

In the morning John took his children to school. When he got home he sorted out his medical kits before starting his shift. His first call was an old man who had fallen downstairs in his home. The old man had a broken arm and two fractured ribs.

His second call was a woman who had a heart attack. They rushed her straight to hospital and she recovered.

His third call was on a building site. A one ton girder had fallen on his leg. The bone inside the leg had snapped in half. They rushed him to hospital. They put a pin in his bone to keep it together.

His fourth call was a lady. A scaffolding pole had fallen on her head. She had concussion, a cracked skull and brain damage. She was immediately rushed to hospital.

His fifth call was a man who had been run over by a lorry. He had concussion, two broken ribs and a broken leg.

His sixth call was a girl who had fallen out of a tree. She had a punctured lung and a broken arm. She was rushed to hospital.

In the evening he finished his shift. He went home to watch telly. He had his dinner then he went to bed.

***Lui Matthews (11)***
***Saxon Primary School***

## HURT

The sun crept through the small gap in my brightly coloured curtains. I rubbed my eyes and thought to myself, 'Another day, another miserable day.'

I walked to school as slowly as possible. I wanted to be late so Matt and his gang wouldn't catch me walking in the school gates. I entered the classroom and sat at my desk. All the lesson I kept thinking about what was coming, what was coming at breaktime? The bell rang. I held my breath and stepped out the door. There was Matt and his gang standing in a huddle at one side of the playground. They approached, I could see Matt's menacing face raging towards me. I closed my eyes. 1, 2, 3, *thump!* I was hit with great force, sending me flying. I curled up in a little ball. They kicked me and gave several more hits, then got bored and walked off.

The pain was unbearable, I wish I could tell someone. But who? They would just get me again. The same thing happened at lunch and after school. I got home at last and ran up into my bedroom and jumped on my bed. That night when my parents had gone to sleep I thought of what would happen the next day. Another beating? I went to sleep. Maybe one day I will find the courage, the courage to stick up for myself.

***Kelly Harris (11)***
***Saxon Primary School***